TARTAN AND MISTLETOE
A HISTORICAL ROMANCE HOLIDAY ANTHOLOGY

JENNIFER ASHLEY

A First-Footer for Lady Jane

Copyright © 2018 by Jennifer Ashley

Fiona and the Three Wise Highlanders

Copyright © 2020 by Jennifer Ashley

These stories are works of fiction. The names, characters, places, and incidents are products of the writer's imagination or have been used fictitiously and are not to be construed as real. Any resemblance to persons, living or dead, actual events, locales or organizations is entirely coincidental.

All Rights are Reserved. No part these stories may be used or reproduced in any manner whatsoever without written permission from the author.

A First-Footer for Lady Jane first appeared in the anthology: *'Tis the Season*, October, 2018

Fiona and the Three Wise Highlanders first appeared in the anthology: *A Very Highland Holiday Collection*, October, 2020

Cover design by Kim Killion

CONTENTS

A FIRST FOOTER FOR LADY JANE	1
FIONA AND THE THREE WISE HIGHLANDERS	59
Also by Jennifer Ashley	151
About the Author	153

A FIRST FOOTER FOR LADY JANE

A REGENCY HOLIDAY ROMANCE

CHAPTER 1

Berkshire, December 31, 1810

"You know precisely whom I will marry, Grandfather. You tease me to enjoy yourself, but all the games in the world will not change that Major Barnett will someday be my husband."

As she spoke, Lady Jane Randolph regarded her grandfather in half amusement, half exasperation. Grandfather MacDonald sprawled in his chair by the fire in the small drawing room in Jane's father's manor house, his blankets in disarray. Grandfather always occupied the warmest place in a room, in deference to his old bones, but he was not one for sitting still.

His lined face held its usual mirth, his blue eyes twinkling. Grandfather MacDonald liked to hint and joke, pretending a connection to the Scottish witches from Macbeth, who, he said, had given him second sight.

"What I say is true, lass." Grandfather fluttered his hands, broad and blunt, which her grandmother, rest her soul, had claimed could brandish a strong sword and then pick out a tune on the harpsichord with such liveliness one could not help but dance. Indeed, Grandfather often sat of an evening at the pianoforte, coaxing rollicking music from it.

Grandfather had been quite a dancer as well, Grandmother had said, and every young woman had vied for a chance to stand up with the swain. When Hamish MacDonald had first cast his eyes upon her, Grandmother had wanted to swoon, but of course she'd never, ever admitted this to him.

"Mark my words," Grandfather went on. "At Hogmanay, the First-Footer over the threshold will marry the most eligible daughter of the house. Hogmanay begins at midnight, and the most eligible young lady in *this* house is you."

"Perhaps." Jane returned to her embroidery, a task she was not fond of. "But you know I already have an agreement with John. No First-Footer need bother with me. There will be other young ladies—Mama and Papa have invited all their acquaintance."

"But you are not yet engaged." Grandfather's eyes sparkled with a wicked light seventy years hadn't dimmed. "No announcement in the newspapers, no date for the happy event, no ring on your finger."

"There is the small matter of war with France." Jane had marred the pattern in her embroidery, she noticed, an inch back. Sighing in annoyance, she picked out the thread. "Major Barnett is a bit busy on the Peninsula just now. When Bonaparte is defeated, there will be plenty of time for happy events."

Silence met her. Jane looked up from repairing her

mistake to find her grandfather glaring at her, his joviality gone.

"Am I hearing ye right?" he demanded. "Ye're discussing your nuptials like ye would decide which field to plant out in the spring. In my day, lassie, we seized the hand of the one who struck our fancy and made sure we hung on to them for life. Didn't matter how many wars we were fighting at the time, and when I was a lad, Highland Scots were being hunted down if we so much as picked up a plaid or spoke our native tongue. Didn't stop Maggie and me running off together, did it?"

Grandfather adored going on about his wild days in the heather, how he and Grandmother never let anything stand in the way of their great passion.

Times had changed, Jane reflected with regret. The war with Napoleon dragged on, the constant worry that France would invade these shores hovering like a distant and evil thunderstorm. She and John must wait until things were resolved—when John came home for good, there would be time enough to make plans for their life together.

The thought that John might never return, that a French artillery shell might end his life, or a bayonet pierce his heart, sent a sudden chill through her.

Jane shuddered and drew a veil over the images. There was no sense in worrying.

She missed another stitch and set the embroidery firmly aside. Grandfather could be most distracting.

"John is in Portugal," she reminded him. "Not likely to be our First-Footer tonight. But someday, perhaps."

"Course he's not likely to be the First-Footer." Grandfather scowled at Jane as though she'd gone simple. "He's a fair-haired man, ain't he? First-Footer needs to be dark. Everyone knows that."

∽

"Your betrothed lives *here*?" Captain Spencer Ingram shook snow from his hat as he climbed from the chaise and gazed at the gabled, rambling, half-timbered monstrosity before him, a holdover from the dark days of knights and bloodthirsty kings.

"Not betrothed," Barnett said quickly. "A childhood understanding. Will lead to an engagement in due time. Probably. Always been that way."

Barnett did not sound as enthusiastic as a man coming home to visit his childhood sweetheart might. Spencer studied his friend, but Barnett's ingenuous face was unconcerned.

Though it was near midnight, every window in the house was lit, and a bonfire leapt high in the night in the fields beyond. Spencer would have preferred wandering to the bonfire, sharing a dram or tankard with villagers no doubt having a dance and a fine time.

The house looked cozy enough, despite its ancient architecture. Lights glowed behind the thick glass windows, welcoming on the frigid evening. The snow was dry and dusty, the night so frozen that no cloud marred the sky. Every star was visible, the carpet of them stretching to infinity. Even better than the bonfire would be a place on the roof and a spyglass through which to gaze at the heavens.

A pair of footmen darted out to seize bags from the compartment in the back of the chaise. Both valises were small, in keeping with soldiers who'd learned to travel with little.

The chaise rattled off toward the stable yard, the driver ready for warmth and a drink. The footmen scurried into the house and disappeared, the front door swinging shut behind them.

Spencer leapt forward to grab the door, but it clanged closed before he reached it.

"What the devil?" Spencer rattled the handle, but the door was now locked. "I call this a poor welcome."

To his surprise, Barnett chuckled. "Lady Jane's family keeps Scots traditions. A visitor arriving after midnight on New Year's—no, we must call it Hogmanay to follow their quaint customs. A visitor arriving after midnight on Hogmanay needs to beg admission, and must bring gifts. I have them here." He held up a canvas sack. "Salt, coal, whisky, shortbread, and black bun."

"Black what?"

"Black bun. A cake of fruit soaked in whisky. It is not bad fare. I obtained the cake from a Scotswoman—the landlord's wife at our accommodations when we first landed."

Spencer had wondered why Barnett insisted on traveling to that inn, well out of the way, the venture taking precious time.

Barnett grinned. "The whole rigmarole is to prove we aren't Norsemen come to pillage the family. 'Tis greatly entertaining, is it not?"

Spencer had other ideas of entertainment. "We stand shivering outside while they decide whether to admit us? There is a good bonfire yonder." He gestured to the fire leaping high in the fields, shadows of revelers around it.

"They'll be waiting just inside. You will see."

Barnett stepped up to the door the footmen had all but slammed in their faces and hammered on it.

"Open, good neighbors. Give us succor." Barnett shot Spencer a merry look. "We must enter into the spirit of the thing."

Spencer heard the bolts rattling, and then the door opened a sliver. "Who is there?" a creaky, elderly man's voice intoned.

"Admit us, good sir." Barnett held the sack aloft. "We bear gifts."

The door opened wider to show a wizened, bent man wrapped in what looked like a long shawl. Spencer sensed several people hovering behind him.

"Then come in, come in. Out of the cold." The man added something in the Scots language Spencer didn't understand and swung the door open.

Barnett started forward, then stopped himself. "No, indeed. You must lead, Spence. A tall, dark-haired man brings the best luck."

He stepped out of the way and more or less shoved Spencer toward the door. Spencer removed his hat and stepped deferentially into the foyer.

Warmth surrounded him, and light. In the silence, he heard a sharp intake of breath.

Beyond the old Scotsman in his plaid shawl, in the doorway to a room beyond, stood a young woman. She was rather tall, but curved, not willowy. Her hair was so dark it was almost black, her eyes, in contrast, a startling blue, like lapis lazuli. They matched the eyes of the old man, but Spencer could no longer see him.

The vision of beauty, in a silk and net gown of shimmering silver, regarded him in alarm but also in wonder.

"Well met, all 'round," Barnett was saying. "Spence, let me introduce you to Lord and Lady Merrickson—the house you are standing in is theirs. Mr. MacDonald, Lady Merrickson's father, and of course, this angel of perfection is Lady Jane Randolph, Lord Merrickson's only daughter and the correspondent that keeps me at ease during the chaos of army life. Lady Jane, may I present Captain Spencer Ingram, the dearest friend a chap could imagine. He saved my life once, you know."

Lady Jane came forward, gliding like a ghost on the wind. Spencer took her hand. Her eyes never left his as he bowed to her, and her lips remained parted with her initial gasp.

Spencer looked at her, and was lost.

CHAPTER 2

*C*aptain Ingram fixed Jane with eyes as gray as winter and as cool, and she couldn't catch her breath. A spark lay deep within those eyes, gleaming like a sunbeam on a flow of ice.

He was not a cold man, though, she knew at once. He was containing his warmth, his animation, being polite. Of course he was—he'd been dragged here by John, likely expecting an ordinary English family at Christmas, only to be thrust into the midst of eccentric Randolphs and MacDonalds.

Jane forced her limbs into a curtsey. "Good evening, Captain Ingram," she said woodenly.

Captain Ingram jerked his gaze to her hand, which he still held, Jane's fingers swallowed by his large gloved ones. Ingram abruptly released her, a bit rudely, she thought, but Jane was too agitated to be annoyed.

"Greet him properly, Jane," Grandfather said. He pushed his way forward, leaning on his stout ash stick, and gave Captain Ingram a nod. "You know how."

Jane swallowed, her jaw tight, and repeated the words Grandfather had taught her years ago. "Welcome, First-Footer. Please partake of our hospitality."

Why was she so unnerved? Grandfather couldn't possibly have predicted that John would step back and let his friend enter the house first, in spite of their conversation earlier today. Grandfather didn't truly have second sight—he only pretended.

Captain Ingram's presence meant nothing, absolutely nothing. After the war, John would propose to Jane, as expected, and life would carry on.

Then why had her heart leapt when she'd beheld Captain Ingram's tall form, why had a sense of gladness and even relief flowed over her? For one instant, she'd believed Grandfather's prediction, and she'd been ... *happy?*

A mad streak ran in Jane's mother's family—or so people said. It was why Grandfather MacDonald spouted the odd things he did, why her mother, a genteel but poor Scotswoman, had been able to ensnare the wealthy Earl of Merrickson, a sought-after bachelor in his younger days. Jane's mother had enchanted him, people said, with her dark hair and intense blue eyes of the inhabitants of the Western Isles. So far, her daughter and son had not yet exhibited the madness of the MacDonald side of the family, thankfully.

Only because Jane, for her part, had learned to hide it, she realized. Given the chance, she'd happily race through the heather in a plaid or dance around a bonfire like the ones the villagers had built tonight. And feel strange glee at the thought she might not marry John after all.

John, oblivious to all tension, hefted a cloth sack. "I've brought the things you told me to, Mr. MacDonald."

"Excellent," Grandfather said. "Jane, take the bag and lay out the treasures in the dining room."

Jane's cousins surged to her. They were the carefree Randolph boys, from her father's side of the family. The three lads, ranging from sixteen to twenty-two, fancied themselves men about town and Corinthians, well pleased that Jane's brother, who was spending New Year's with his wife's family, stood between themselves and the responsibility of the earldom. In truth, they were harmless, though mischievous.

"Come, come, come, Cousin Jane," the youngest, Thomas, sang as they led the way to the dining room.

Jane took the bag from John, trying to pay no attention to Captain Ingram, who had not stepped away from her. "How are you, John? How very astonishing to see you."

John winked at her. He had blue eyes and light blond hair, the very picture of an English gentleman. "Amazing to me when we got leave, wasn't it, Spence? Thought I'd surprise you, Janie. Worked, didn't it? You look pole-axed."

Jane clutched the bag to her chest, finding it difficult to form words. "I beg your pardon. I am shocked, is all. Did not expect you."

John sent Captain Ingram a grin. "*I beg your pardon*, she says, all prim and proper. She didn't used to be so. You ought to have seen her running bare-legged through the meadows, screaming like a savage with me, her brother, and her cousins."

Jane went hot. "When I was seven."

"And eight, and nine, and ten ... until you were seventeen, I imagine. How old are you now, Janie? I've forgotten."

"Twenty," Jane said with dignity.

"Mind your tongue, Barnett," Captain Ingram broke in with a scowl. "Lady Jane might forgive your ill-mannered question, as our journey was long and arduous, but I would not blame her if she did not. Allow me to carry that for you, my lady."

He reached for the bag, which Jane relinquished, it being rather heavy, and strode with it into the dining room where the rest of the family had streamed.

"He's gallant that way," John said without rancor. "I knew you'd approve of him. You've grown very pretty, Jane."

"Thank you," Jane said, awkward. "You've grown very frank."

"That's the army for you. You enter a stiff and callow youth and emerge a hot-blooded and crude man. I crave pardon for my jokes. Have I upset you?"

"No, indeed," she said quickly.

In truth, Jane wasn't certain. John was changed—he had been, as he said, stiff and overly polite when he'd come out of university and taken a commission in the army. This grinning buffoon was more like the boy she'd known in her youth.

John offered her his arm. "Shall we?"

Jane acquiesced, and John propelled her into the dining room. The cousins had already emptied the sack and now sifted through its contents with much hilarity.

"A lump of coal—that's for you, Thomas." His oldest

brother threw it at him, and Thomas caught it good-naturedly.

"Excellent fielding," John said. "Do you all still play cricket?"

"We do," Thomas said, and the cousins went off on a long aside about cricket games past and present.

Lord Merrickson roared at them to cease, though without rancor. Lady Merrickson greeted John and Captain Ingram with a warm smile. John took on the cross-eyed, smitten look he always wore in front of Jane's mother. Jane did not believe him in love with her mother, exactly, but awed by her. Many gentlemen were.

Captain Ingram, on the other hand, was deferential and polite to Lady Merrickson, as was her due, but nothing more.

As Ingram moved back to Jane, she noted that his greatcoat was gone—taken by one of the footmen. His uniform beneath, the deep blue of a cavalryman, held the warmth of his body.

He leaned to her. "Do they ever let you insert a word?" he asked quietly.

Jane tried not to shiver at his voice's low rumble. "On occasion," she said. "I play a fine game of cricket myself. Or used to. As John said, I am much too prim and proper now."

"No, she ain't," the middle Randolph cousin, Marcus, proclaimed. "Just this summer she hiked up her petticoats and took up the bat."

"A pity I missed it," John said loudly. "We ought to scare up a team of ladies at camp, Ingram. Officers wives versus …"

Marcus and Thomas burst out laughing, and the

oldest cousin, Digby, looked aghast. "I say, old chap. Not in front of Jane."

"Your pardon, Jane." John looked anything but sorry. He was unusually merry tonight. Perhaps he'd imbibed a quantity of brandy to stave off the cold of the journey.

"I am not offended," Jane answered. "But my mother might be."

Lady Merrickson was not at all, Jane knew, but the admonition made John flush. "Er …" he spluttered.

"Whisky!" Digby snatched up the bottle and held it high. "Thank you, John. All is forgiven. Marcus, fetch the glasses. Mr. MacDonald, the black bun is for you, I think."

Grandfather snatched up the cake wrapped in muslin and held it to his nose. "A fine one. Like me old mum used to bake."

Grandfather's "old mum" had a cook to do her baking, so Jane had been told. His family had lived well in the Highlands before the '45.

Outside, the piper Grandfather had hired began to drone, the noise of the pipes wrapping around the house.

"What the devil is *that*?" John demanded.

"I believe they are bagpipes," Captain Ingram said. His mild tone made Jane want to laugh. "You have heard them in the Highland regiments."

"Not like that. Phew, what a racket."

Grandfather scowled at him. "Ye wouldn't know good piping from a frog croaking, lad. There are fiddlers and drummers waiting in the ballroom. Off we go."

The cousins, with whisky and glasses, pounded out of the dining room and along the hall to the ballroom in the back of the house. John escorted Jane, hurrying her to the entertainment, while Captain Ingram politely walked with Grandfather. The terrace windows in the ballroom framed the bonfires burning merrily a mile or so away.

Three musicians waited, two with fiddles, one with a drum. They struck up a Scottish tune as the family entered, blending with the piper outside.

Guest who'd been staying at the house and those arriving now that the First-Footer ritual was done swarmed around them. They were neighbors and old friends of the family, and soon laughter and chatter filled the room.

Grandfather spoke a few moments with Captain Ingram, then he threw off his shawl and cane and jigged to the drums and fiddles, cheered on by Jane's cousins and John. Ingram, politely accepting a whisky Digby had thrust at him, watched with interest.

"I am not certain this was the welcome you expected," Jane said when she drifted near him again.

"It will do." Ingram looked down at her, his gray eyes holding fire. "Is every New Year like this for you?"

"I am afraid so," Jane answered. "Grandfather insists."

"He enjoys it, I'd say."

Grandfather kicked up his heels, a move that made him totter, but young Thomas caught him, and the two locked arms and whirled away.

"He does indeed." Some considered Jane's grandfather a foolish old man, but he had more life in him than many insipid young aristocrats she met during the London Season.

The music changed to that of a country dance, and

couples formed into lines, ladies facing gentlemen. John immediately went to a young lady who was the daughter of Jane's family's oldest friends and led her out.

"Lady Jane?" Ingram offered his arm. "I am an indifferent dancer, but I will make the attempt."

Jane did not like the way her heart fluttered at the sight of Captain Ingram's hard arm, outlined by the tight sleeve of his coat. Jane was as good as betrothed—she should not have to worry about her heart fluttering again.

Out of nowhere, Jane felt cheated. Grandfather's stories of his courtship with her grandmother, filled with passion and romance, flitted through her mind. The two had been very much in love, had run away together to the dismay of both families, and then defied them all and lived happily ever after. For one intense moment, Jane wanted that.

Such a foolish idea. Better to marry the son of a neighbor everyone approved of. Prudence and wisdom lined the path to true happiness.

Jane gazed at Captain Ingram, inwardly shaking more than she had the first time she'd fallen from a horse. Flying through the air, not knowing where she'd land, had both terrified and exhilarated her.

"I do not wish to dance," she said. Captain Ingram's expression turned to disappointment, but Jane put her hand on his sleeve. "Shall we walk out to the bonfires instead?"

The longing in his eyes was unmistakable. The captain had no wish to be shut up in a hot ballroom with people he didn't know. Jane had no wish to be here either.

Freedom beckoned.

Captain Ingram studied Jane a moment, then he nodded in resolve. "I would enjoy that, yes."

Jane led him from the ballroom, her heart pounding, wondering, as she had that day she'd been flung from her mare's back, if her landing would be rough or splendid.

CHAPTER 3

*A*s much as he wished to, Spencer could not simply rush into the night alone with Lady Jane. Such a thing was not done. Lady Jane bade two footmen, who fetched Jane's and Spencer's wraps, to bundle up and accompany them with lanterns. The lads, eager to be out, set forth, guiding the way into the darkness.

Five people actually tramped to the bonfires, because the youngest of the cousins, Thomas, joined them at the last minute.

"You're saving me," Thomas told Spencer as he fell into step with them. "Aunt Isobel wants me standing up with debutantes, as though I'd propose to one tomorrow. I ain't marrying for a long while, never fear. I want to join the army, like you."

"Army life is harsh, Mr. Randolph," Spencer said. "Unmerciful hours, drilling in all weather, not to mention French soldiers shooting at you."

"Not afraid of the Frenchies," Thomas proclaimed.

"Tell him, Janie. I want to be off. I'll volunteer if Uncle won't buy me a commission."

"He does speak of it day and night," Lady Jane said. She walked along briskly but not hurriedly, as though the cold did not trouble her at all. "Do not paint too romantic a picture of army life, please, Captain, or you might find him in your baggage when you go."

"Perhaps Major Barnett should speak to him as a friend of the family," Spencer said, trying to make his tone diffident.

Jane laughed, a sound like music. "It is Major Barnett's fault Thomas wants to be a soldier in the first place. John writes letters full of his bravado. Also of the fine meals he has with his commanding officers, and the balls he attends, which are full of elegant ladies."

Spencer hid his irritation. Lady Jane held a beauty that had struck him to the bone from the moment he'd beheld her—her dark hair and azure eyes more suited to a faery creature floating in the mists of a loch than a young miss dwelling on a country farm in the middle of England.

If Spencer had been fortunate enough to have such a lady waiting for him, he'd write letters describing how he pined for her, not ones about meals with his colonel and wife. As far as Spencer knew, Barnett did not have a mistress, but he did enjoy dancing and chattering with the officers' wives and daughters. Man was an ingrate.

Barnett had mentioned the daughter of his father's closest neighbor on occasion, but not often. Never rejoiced in receiving her letters, never treasured them or read bits out. Nor hinted, with a blush, that he couldn't *possibly* read them out loud.

He'd only spoken the name Lady Jane Randolph that Spencer could remember a few weeks ago, when he'd announced he'd be returning to England for New Year's. He'd obtained leave and had for Spencer as well.

Spencer had been ready to go. Melancholia commanded him much of late, as he saw his future stretching before him, bleak and grim. If he did not end up dead on a battlefield with French bullets inside him, he would continue life as a junior officer without many prospects. Bonaparte was tough to wedge from the Peninsula—he'd already taken over most of the Italian states and much of the Continent, and had his relatives ruling corners of his empire for him. Only England and Portugal held out, and there was nothing to say Portugal would not fall.

Even if Napoleon was defeated, there was noise of coming war in America. Spencer would either continue the slog in the heat and rain of Portugal or be shipped off to the heat and rain of the New World.

Even if Spencer sold his commission in a few years, as he planned, what then? He itched to see the world—not in an army tent or charging his horse across a battlefield, but properly, on the Grand Tour he'd missed because of war. But Bonaparte was everywhere.

More likely, Spencer would go home and learn to run the estate he'd eventually inherit. He didn't like to think of *that* day either, because it would mean his beloved father had died.

John Barnett, rising quickly through the ranks, courtesy of familial influence, had this beautiful woman to return to whenever he chose, one with a large and friendly family in the soft Berkshire countryside.

And the idiot rarely spoke of her, preferring to flirt with the colorless daughters of his colonels and generals.

If Bonaparte's soldiers didn't shoot Barnett, Spencer might.

The village was a mile from the house down a straight road, easy to navigate on a fine night, but Spencer shivered.

"Are you well, Captain Ingram?" Lady Jane asked in concern. "Perhaps we shouldn't have come out. You must be tired from your travels. Holidays are not pleasant when one has a cold."

"I am quite well," Spencer answered, trying to sound cheerful. "I was reflecting how peaceful it all is. Safe." No sharpshooters waiting to take out stragglers, no pockets of French soldiers to capture and torture one. Only starlight, a quiet if icy breeze, a thin blanket of white snow, a lovely woman walking beside him, and warm firelight to beckon them on.

"Yes, it is. Safe." Lady Jane sounded discontented.

"Janie longs for adventure," Thomas confided. "Like me."

"I, on the other hand, believe this a perfect night," Spencer said, his spirits rising. "Companionship, conversation. Beauty."

Thomas snorted with laughter, but Spencer saw Jane's polite smile fade.

At that moment, village children ran to envelope them and drag them to the bonfire.

The footmen eagerly joined friends and family around the blazes. A stoneware jug made its rounds to men and women alike, and voices rose in song.

Jane released Spence's arm, the cold of her absence

disheartening. She beamed in true gladness as village women greeted her and pulled her into their circle.

Spencer watched Lady Jane come alive, the primness she'd exhibited in her family home dropping away. Her face blossomed in the firelight, a midnight curl dropped to her shoulder, and her eyes sparkled like starlight—his faery creature in a fur-lined redingote and bonnet.

Barnett has a lot to answer for, he thought in disgust. *She deserves so much more.*

But who was Spencer to interfere with his friend's intentions? Perhaps Barnett loved her dearly and was too bashful to say so.

The devil he was. When Barnett had greeted Jane tonight, he'd betrayed no joy of at last being with her, no need for her presence. He was as obtuse as a brick. Barnett had Jane safely in his sights, and took for granted she'd always be there.

Man needed to be taught a lesson. Spencer decided then and there to be the teacher.

∽

JANE HAD FORGOTTEN HOW MUCH SHE ENJOYED THE bonfires at New Year's. The villagers had always had a New Year's celebration, and when Grandfather came to live with Jane's family after Grandmother's death, he'd taught them all about Hogmanay. None of the villagers were Scots, and in fact, had ancestors who'd fought Bonnie Prince Charlie, but the lads and lasses of Shefford St. Mary were always keen for a knees-up.

Jane had come to the bonfires every year as a child with her brother and cousins, and tonight, she was welcomed by the village women with smiles, curtseys, and even embraces.

The villagers linked hands to form a ring around one of the fires. Jane found her hand enclosed in Captain Ingram's large, warm one, his grip firm under his glove. Thomas clasped her other hand and nearly dragged Jane off her feet as they began to circle the fire at a rapid pace.

She glanced at Captain Ingram, to find his gray eyes fixed on her, his smile broad and genuine. His reserve evaporated as the circle continued, faster and faster. He'd claimed to be an indifferent dancer, but in wild abandon, he excelled.

Jane found she did too. Before long, she was laughing out loud, kicking up her feet as giddily as Grandfather had, as the villagers snaked back and forth. This was true country dancing, not the orchestrated, rather stiff parading in the ballroom.

The church clocks in this village and the next struck two, the notes shimmering in the cold. Village men seized their sweethearts, their wives, swung them around, and kissed them.

Strong hands landed on Jane's waist. Captain Ingram pulled her in a tight circle, out of the firelight. A warm red glow brushed his face as he dragged Jane impossibly close. Then he kissed her.

The world spun, silence taking the place of laughter, shouting, the crackle of the fire, the dying peal of the bells.

Spencer Ingram's heat washed over Jane, dissolving anything stiff, until she flowed against him, her lips seeking his.

The kiss was tender, a brief moment of longing, of

desire simmering below the surface. Jane wanted that moment to stretch forever, through Hogmanay night to welcoming dawn, and for the rest of her life.

Revelers bumped them, and Spencer broke the kiss. Jane hung in his arms, he holding her steady against the crush.

She saw no remorse in his eyes, no shame that he'd kissed another man's intended. Jane felt no remorse either. She was a free woman, not officially betrothed, not yet belonging to John, and she knew this with all her being.

Spencer set her on her feet and gently released her. They continued to study each other, no words between them, only acknowledgment that they had kissed, and that it had meant something.

Thomas came toward them. "We should go back, Janie," he said with regret. "Auntie will be looking for us."

He seemed to have noticed nothing, not the kiss, not the way Jane and Spencer regarded each other in charged silence.

The moment broke. Jane turned swiftly to Thomas and held out her hand. "Yes, indeed. It is high time we went home."

∼

"A BONE TO PICK." SPENCER CLOSED THE DOOR OF THE large room where Barnett amused himself alone at a billiards table in midmorning sunlight. His eyes were red-rimmed from last night's revelry, but he greeted Spencer with a cheerful nod.

"Only if you procure a cue and join me."

Spencer chose a stout but slender stick from the cabinet and moved to the table as Barnett positioned a red ball on its surface and rolled a white toward Spencer.

Spencer closed his hand over the ball and spun it toward the other end of the table at the same time Barnett did his. Both balls bounced off the cushions and rolled back toward them, Spencer's coming to rest closer to its starting point than Barnett's. Therefore, Spencer's choice as to who went first.

He spread his hands and took a step back. "By all means."

Spencer was not being kind—the second player often had the advantage.

He remained politely silent as Barnett began taking his shots. He was a good player, his white ball kissing the red before the white dropped into a pocket, often clacking against Spencer's white ball as well. Spencer obligingly fished out balls each time so Barnett could continue racking up points.

Only when Barnett fouled out by his white ball missing the red by a hair and coming to rest in the middle of the table did Spencer speak.

"I must tell you, Barnett, that I find your treatment of Lady Jane appalling."

Barnett blinked and straightened from grimacing at his now-motionless ball. "I beg your pardon? I wasn't aware I'd been appalling to the dear gel."

"You've barely spoken to her at all. I thought this was the lady you wanted to marry."

Barnett nodded. "Suppose I do."

"You *suppose*? She is a beautiful woman, full of fire,

with the finest eyes I've ever seen, and you *suppose* you wish to marry her?"

"Well, it's never been settled one way or another. We are of an age, grew up together. Really we are the only two eligible people for miles. We all used to play together—Jane, her brother, her cousins, me." Barnett laughed. "I remember once when we dared her to climb the face of Blackbird Hill, a steep, rough rock, and she did it. And once—"

Spencer cut him off with a sweep of his hand. "A spirited girl, yes. And now a spirited woman fading while she waits for you to say a word. She's halting her life because everyone expects you to propose. It's cruel to her to hesitate. Criminal even."

"Jove, you are in a state." Barnett idly took up chalk and rubbed it on the tip of his cue. He leaned to take a shot, remembered he'd lost his turn, and rose again. "What do you wish me to do? Propose to her, today?" He looked as though this were the last thing on earth he'd wish to do.

"No, I believe you should let her go. If you don't wish to marry her, tell her so. End her uncertainty."

"Hang on. Are you saying Jane is pining for me?" Barnett grinned. "How delicious."

Spencer slammed his cue to the table. "I am saying you've trapped her. She feels obligated to you because of family expectations, while you go your merry way. Your flirtations at camp border on courtship, and I assumed your intended was a dull wallflower you were avoiding. Now that I've met her ... You're an idiot, Barnett."

"Now, look here, Ingram. *Captain*."

"You outrank me in the field, *sir*. In civilian life, no.

Lady Jane is a fine young woman who does not need to be tied to you. Release her, let her find a suitor in London this Season, let her make her own choice."

Barnett's mouth hung open during Spence's speech, and now he closed it with a snap. "Her own choice—do you mean someone like *you*?"

Spencer scowled at him. "First of all, your tone is insulting. Second, when I say her own choice, I mean it. Cease forcing her to wait for you to come home, to speak. Let her begin her life."

Barnett laid down his cue with exaggerated care. "Very well. I suppose you pulling me away from that Frenchie's bayonet gives you some leave to speak to me so. Happen I might propose to her this very day. Will that gain your approval?"

Not at all. Spencer had hoped to make Barnett realize he didn't care for Lady Jane, never had, not as anything more than a childhood friend.

The man who proposed to Jane should be wildly in love with her, ready to do anything to make her life perfect and happy. She should have no less.

When Spencer had kissed her—

The frivolous, New Year's kiss had instantly changed to one of intense desire. Need had struck Spencer so hard he'd barely been able to remain standing. He'd wanted to hold on to Jane and run with her to Scotland, to jump the broomstick with her before anyone could stop them.

She never would. Spencer already understood that Jane had a deep sense of obligation, which she'd thrown off to dance in the firelight last night, like the wild thing she truly was. But today, she'd be back to responsibility.

He hadn't seen her this morning, not at breakfast, which he'd rushed to anxiously, nor moving about the house, and he feared she'd decided to remain in her rooms and avoid him.

Spencer did not know what he'd say to her when she appeared. But he refused to put the kiss behind him, to pretend it never happened.

He didn't want Jane to pretend it hadn't happened either. He'd seen in her eyes the yearnings he felt—for love, for life, for something beyond what each of them had.

Spencer faced Barnett squarely. "Do not propose to her," he said. "Do not force her to plunge further into obligation. She won't refuse you. She'll feel it her duty to accept."

"It is her duty, damn you. What am I to do? Leave her for you?" When Spencer didn't answer, Barnett's eyes widened. "I see. Devil take you, man. I brought you home as a friend."

Spencer held him with a gaze that made Barnett's color rise. "That is true. Are you going to call me out?"

Barnett hesitated, then shook his head. "I'll not sully our friendship by falling out over a woman."

Spencer fought down disgust. "If you loved her, truly loved her, you'd strike me down for even daring to suggest I wanted her, and then you'd leap over my body and rush to her. You don't love her, do you? Not with all your heart."

Barnett shrugged. "Well, I'm fond of the gel, naturally."

"*Fond* is not what I'd feel, deep inside my soul, for the woman I wanted to spend the rest of my life with."

Spencer slapped his palm to his chest. "Release her, Barnett. Or love her, madly, passionately. She merits no less than that."

Spencer seized his white ball and spun it across the table. It caromed off one edge, two, three, and then struck the red ball with a crack like a gunshot and plunged into a pocket.

"Add up my points," Spencer said. "If you will not tell Lady Jane what is truly in your heart, *I* will."

He strode from the room, his heart pounding, his blood hot. *The captain is a volatile man,* he'd heard his commanders say of him, *Once he sets his mind on a thing, step out of his way.*

Behind him, Barnett called plaintively, "What about the game? I'll have to consider it a forfeit, you know."

A forfeit, indeed.

Spencer went down the stairs to the main hall and asked the nearest footman to direct him to Lady Jane.

CHAPTER 4

The gardens were covered with snow, the fountains empty and silent, but they suited Jane's mood. She ought to be in the house entertaining guests, or helping her mother, or looking after Grandfather, but she could not behave as though nothing had shaken her life to its foundations.

She should be glad John was home, feel tender happiness as the reward for waiting for his return.

All she could think of was Spencer Ingram's gray eyes sparkling in the firelight after he'd kissed her. Could think only of the heat of his lips on hers, the fiery touch of his tongue. It was as though John Barnett did not exist.

Was she so fickle? So featherheaded that the moment another man crossed her path, she eagerly turned to follow him?

Or was there more than that? John had more or less ignored her since he'd arrived. Instead of resenting his indifference, Jane had been relieved.

Relieved. What was the matter with her?

A pair of statues at the far end of the garden marked the edge of her father's park. Both statues were of Hercules—the one the right battling the Nemean lion; on the left, the hydra. Beyond these guardians lay pastureland rolling to far hills, today covered with a few inches of snow.

Jane contemplated the uneven land beyond the statues and reluctantly turned to tramp back.

A man in a blue uniform with greatcoat and black boots strode around the fountains and empty flower beds toward her. He was alone, and his trajectory would make him intersect Jane's path. No one else wandered the garden, few bold enough to risk the ice-cold January morning.

Running would look foolish, not to mention Jane had nowhere to go. The fields, cut by a frozen brook, offered hazardous footing. Plus she was cold and ready to return to the house. Why should she flee her own father's garden?

Jane continued resolutely toward Captain Ingram, nodding at him as they neared each other. "Good morning," she said neutrally.

"Good morning," he echoed, halting before her. "Is it good?"

Jane curled her fingers inside her fur muff. "The weather is fair, the sun shining. The guests are enjoying themselves. The New Year's holiday is always pleasant."

Ingram's eyes narrowed. "Pleasant. Enjoying themselves." His voice held a bite of anger. "What about you, Lady Jane? Are you enjoying yourself?"

"Of course. I like to see everyone home. If my

brother and his wife could come, that would be even more splendid."

"Liar."

Jane started, her heart beating faster, but she kept her tone light. "I beg your pardon? I truly do long to see my brother."

"You are miserable and cannot wait for the morning Major Barnett and I ride away."

Jane lost her forced smile. "You are rude."

"I am. Many say this of me. But I am a plain speaker and truthful." His gray eyes glinted as he fixed an unrelenting gaze on her. "Tell me why the devil you are tying yourself to Barnett."

Why? There was every reason why—Jane simply had never thought the reasons through. "I have known him a very long time …"

Spencer stepped closer to her. "If you were madly in love with him, you'd have slapped me silly when I tried to kiss you, last night. Instead you joined me."

Jane rested her muff against her chest, as though it would shield her. "Are you casting my folly up to me? Not very gentlemanly of you."

To her surprise, Spencer smiled, his anger transforming to heat. It was a feral smile, the fierceness in his eyes making her tremble.

"*I* am the fool for kissing you," he said in a hard voice. "I couldn't help myself. I think no less of you for kissing me back. In fact, I have been rejoicing all night and morning that you did. Haven't slept a bloody wink."

Jane swallowed. "Neither have I, as a matter of fact."

"Then you give me hope. Much hope."

He took another step to her, and Jane feared he would kiss her again.

Feared? Or desired it?

She pulled back, but not because he frightened her. She stepped away because she wanted very much to kiss him, properly this time. She'd fling her arms around him and drag him close, enjoying the warmth of him against her.

She touched the muff to her lips, the fur tickling.

Spencer laughed. "You are beautiful, Lady Jane. And enchanting. A wild spirit barely tamed by a respectable dress and winter coat."

"Hardly a wild spirit." Jane moved the muff to speak. "I embroider—not well, I admit—paint watercolors rather better, and help my mother keep house."

"Your grandfather told me stories of himself and your grandmother last night. You are much like her."

Jane wanted to think so. Maggie MacDonald, what Jane remembered of her, had been a laughing, happy woman, given to telling frightening stories of ghosts that haunted the Highlands or playing games with her grandchildren. She also loved to dance. Jane had a memory of her donning a man's kilt and performing a sword dance as gracefully and adeptly as any warrior. Grandfather had watched her with love in his eyes.

"She was a grand woman," Jane said softly. "I can't begin to compare to her."

"She is in your blood." Spencer took another step, pushing the muff downward. "I saw that when we were at the fire. You were free, happy. I will stand here until you admit it."

"I was." Jane could not lie, even to herself. "Last night, I was happy."

"But this morning, you have convinced yourself you must be this other Jane. Dutiful. Tethered. *Un*happy."

Jane ducked from him and started toward the statues at the end of the garden. She had no idea why she did not rush to the house instead—Hercules was far too busy with his own struggles to help her.

Unhappy. Yes, she was. But that was hardly his business.

She heard Spencer's boots on the snow-covered gravel behind her and swung to face him. "Why do you follow me, sir? If I am miserable, perhaps I wish to console myself in solitude."

"Because I want to be with you." Spencer halted a foot from her. "There, I have declared myself. I want to be with you, and no other. I do not care one whit that you and Barnett have an understanding. He is not in love with you—I can see that. Such news might hurt you, but you must know the truth."

It did hurt. Jane had grown complacent about her friendship with John, pleased she could live without worry for her future, thankful she had no need to chase gentlemen during her Season and could simply enjoy London's many entertainments. She assisted other ladies to find husbands instead of considering them rivals.

Spencer's arrival had shattered her complacency, and now its shards lay around her.

She fought to maintain her composure. "Are you suggesting I throw over Major Barnett and declare myself for you?"

"Nothing would make me happier."

Spencer leaned close, and again, Jane thought he'd kiss her. Anything sensible spun out of her head as she anticipated the brush of his lips, the warmth of his touch. He came closer still, his gaze darting to her mouth, his chest rising sharply. Jane's very breath hurt.

When he straightened, disappointment slapped her.

"Nothing would make me happier," Spencer repeated. "But I'm not a blackguard. If you have no regard for me, if you cannot imagine yourself loving me, then I will not press you. I won't press you at all. What I want, my dear lady, is your happiness. I know in my heart it does not lie for you with Major Barnett."

Jane shook her head. "The world is convinced it does."

"Then the world is a fool. I would be the happiest man alive if you chose me. But I won't ask you to, won't coerce you." His dark brows came down. "I want you to be free, Jane. Free to choose. Go to London. Have your Season—laugh, dance, *live*. If you find a better man than I there, then I'll … well, I'll sink into despondency for a long while, but that despondency will have a bright note. I'll know you are happy. Find that man, and I will dance at your wedding. I promise."

Her breath came fast. "You amaze me, sir."

"Why?" Again a smile, bright and hot. "I admire you. I hate to see you pressed into a box, your nature stifled, all because of an ass like Major Barnett."

Jane attempted a frown. "Should I throw off my friends the moment they displease me? Is this freedom?" Her voice shook, because in her heart, his words made her sing.

"You know Barnett has been displeasing you for

years," Spencer said. "Else you'd have looked happier to see him."

Truth again. Was this man an oracle?

"How dare you?" Jane tried to draw herself up, but her question lacked conviction. Spencer unnerved her, turned her inside out, made her want to laugh and cry. "This is none of your affair, sir."

She ought to threaten to call her father, have Captain Ingram ejected from the house, even arrested for accosting her. Or she could simply slap him, as he'd told her she should have done last night.

Spencer's gaze held her, and Jane could do nothing.

"It is my affair because I care about you," he said. "But *I* do not matter. You do. Please, Jane, be happy."

Blast him. Before he'd arrived, Jane's life had been tranquil. At ease. Now confusion pounded at her, and shame.

Because she knew good and well she hadn't been tranquil at all. She'd been impatient, angry. Stifled, as he said.

Spencer's eyes held anguish, rage, and need. Jane knew somehow that Spencer Ingram would always speak truth to her, whether she liked it or not.

And she knew she wanted to kiss him again.

The house was far away, and high yew hedges edged the path on which they stood. No one was about, not even a gardener taking a turn around the empty beds. Most of the servants had been given a holiday.

Jane took the last step toward Spencer. As he regarded her in both trepidation and simmering need, Jane wrapped her arms around his neck and kissed him.

His lips were parted, his breath heating hers an

instant before he hauled her against him, his answering kiss hard, savage.

The world melted away. All Jane knew was Spencer's solid, strong body, his hands holding her steady, his mouth on hers.

He pulled her closer, the tall length of him hard against her softness. His lips opened hers, mouth seeking, whiskers scratching her cheek. He filled up everything empty inside her, and Jane learned warmth, joy, longing.

We never let anything stand in the way of us, Grandfather always said about himself and his beloved Maggie.

That was long ago, Jane would reason.

But *this* was now.

Jane abruptly broke the kiss. Spencer gazed at her, desire plain in his eyes. He traced her cheek, and her heart shattered.

Jane drew away from him, and ran. She snatched up the freedom he offered her and sprinted down the main path, her arms open, muff hanging from one hand, and let the cold air come.

∽

"John, may I have a word?"

Jane was surprised she had breath left after her mad dash through the garden. She'd taken time to shed her outdoor things and compose herself before she sought John.

She found him in the library, book in hand, but he wasn't reading. John gazed rather wistfully out the window to the park in front of the house, the book dangling idly.

When he heard Jane, he rose to his feet and pasted on a polite smile. "Good morning, Jane. Did you have a nice walk?"

Jane halted, her cheeks scalding. Had he seen the kiss? Or been told about it?

John's face, however, held the bland curiosity of a man who had been thinking of everything but Jane, only recalled to her existence by her presence.

"The walk was agreeable," Jane said hastily. She glanced behind her to make certain the few servants who'd agreed to stay and help today did not linger in the hall. She dared not close the door in case a guest insisted that Jane shut into a room with her old friend meant either her ruin or their engagement.

She had no idea how to begin, so she jumped to the point, bypassing politeness.

"John, I would take it kindly if you did not propose to me."

John stared at her as though he didn't understand her words, then his brows climbed, his mouth forming a half smile. "I beg your pardon?"

Jane balled her hands and plunged on. "Please do not propose marriage to me. It will be easier for both of us if I do not have to refuse you."

CHAPTER 5

"Oh." John gaped at her. His features were still very like those he'd had as a child—round cheeks, soft chin, bewildered brown eyes. "Damn and blast—Ingram has got at you, has he? Viper to my bosom."

"Captain Ingram?" Good heavens, had Spencer discussed this with John? "Captain Ingram has nothing to do with this," Jane said heatedly. "Or, if he does, it is that he made me see keeping silent is hurting you as well as myself. We do not care for each other—not in the 'til-death-do-us-part fashion, in any case. Of course I have affection for you as a friend, and always will. We grew up together. But that does not mean we should continue as man and wife, no matter how many members of our family and friends believe so."

John's astonishment grew as Jane rambled, and she trailed off, her face unbearably hot.

John lifted his chin. "I cannot believe you so flighty,

Jane, that you could allow a man, who pretends to be a gentleman, change your thoughts so swiftly."

"He did not." Jane shook her head, her heart squeezing. "I've had these thoughts a long time, even if I did not admit them to myself. But I did not want to hurt you, my dear old friend. I believe now that *not* speaking will do even more harm. What happens if, in a year or two, you meet a lady you truly love? One who could be your helpmeet, your friend, the mother of your children? And you were already betrothed or married to me? Let us prevent that tragedy here and now."

John scowled. "Or is it that *you* wish to fall in love with another and not be tied to *me*?"

"Nonsense," Jane said. "I have no intention of marrying anyone."

She flushed even as she spoke. Spencer tempted her, yes, but she barely knew him. She would not fly from an understanding with John to an elopement with Spencer in the space of a day.

Would she?

"I believe you," John said in a hard voice. "Your nose held so high, your frosty demeanor in place. You've grown cold, Jane. If I haven't spoken to you about sharing a stall for life, it is because you are quite disagreeable these days. Your letters to me are so formal, about what calves were born and who danced with whom at the village ball. Enthralling."

Jane's coolness evaporated in a flash. "These in answer to the very few letters you have sent *me*. I've not heard from you since summer, in fact. Do not bother to use the excuse of battles, because your mother has had plenty of letters from you, as has my brother, and I know that the sister of a man in your regiment has heard plenty from *him* — the letters arrive in England on the same ship. But none from you to me."

John reddened. "Hardly seemly, is it, writing to a lady to whom I am not engaged?"

"It did not stop you the first year you were gone, nor has it stopped you scolding me for not writing scintillating letters to you."

John attempted a lofty tone. "You are such a child, Jane."

"No, I am not. I am twenty, as I reminded you last night, older than several ladies of my acquaintance who are already married. Old enough to be on the shelf, as you know. But I will not tie us to a marriage neither of us wants to avoid that fate."

"Ah, so that is why you were always sweet to me, eh, Janie? So you'd never be an ape-leader?" John's mouth pinched. "I'll have you know that I planned to speak to you this week, my dear, but not to propose. To tell you there is the sister of an officer who has caught my eye, and as you have become so cool, and she is quite warm, that we should agree to part."

Jane's heart stung, and she regarded him in remorse. She hadn't wanted to anger John, but how could he not be angry? His stabs at her came from his bafflement and hurt, but Jane sensed that he was more insulted at her refusal than deeply wounded.

John would return to his regiment and happily court the officer's sister, and forget he ever had feelings for Jane. In fact, John had behaved, since his arrival, as though he'd forgotten those feelings already.

Hopefully, in time, John would forgive her, and

they'd continue as friends, as they had been all their lives. But friends with no obligation attached.

"Good-bye, John," Jane said, and quietly walked out of the room.

∽

Spencer did not see Jane the rest of the day. He walked through the gardens, the park, the woods, then took a horse and went on a long ride. It was snowing by the time he returned, and dark.

He did not see Barnett either, which was a mercy. Spencer then realized he'd seen no one at all as he returned to his chamber. He washed and changed and descended in search of supper, but the residents of the house were elusive. Where had they all gone?

"Hurry up, lad," a voice with a Scottish lilt said to him. "You're the last."

"The last for what, sir?" Spencer asked Lady Jane's grandfather as the elderly man tottered to him.

"The hunt, of course. Here's your list. You're with Thomas and my daughter. Off you go."

Spencer gazed down at a paper with a jumble of items written on it: A flat iron, a locket, a horseshoe, a thimble, and a dozen more bizarre things that did not match.

"What is this?" he asked in bewilderment.

"A scavenger hunt, slow-top. The first team to gather the things wins a prize. Go on with ye."

Spencer hesitated. "Where is Jane? Lady Jane, that is."

"With the older cousins and a friend from down the lane. Why are you still standing here?"

"The thing is, sir, I … I'm not sure who to speak to …"

The old Scotsman waved him away, his plaids swinging. "Aye, I know all about it. Give the lass time to settle, and she'll come 'round. She only gave Major Barnett the elbow a few hours ago."

Spencer's heart leapt. "She did?"

"Yes. Thank the Lord. Now, hurry away. Enjoy yourself while you're still young."

Spencer grinned in sudden hope. "Yes, sir. Of course, sir."

As he dashed away, he heard Grandfather MacDonald muttering behind him. "In my day, I'd have already put the girl over my shoulder and run off with her. Otherwise, she'd not think I was sincere."

∾

Jane handed her spoils—a blue beaded slipper, a quizzing glass, and a small rolling pin—to her cousin Digby, and slipped into the chamber she'd spied her grandfather ducking into. The small anteroom was covered with paintings her father's father had collected. A strange place for Grandfather MacDonald to hide—he believed Van Dyke and Rubens over-praised. Only Scottish painters like Allan Ramsay and Henry Raeburn had ever been any good.

"Grandfather."

Grandfather looked up from a settee, where he'd

been nodding off, but his eyes were bright, alert. He came to his feet.

"Yes, my dear? Are you well?"

"No." Jane sank down to a painted silk chair. "Everything is turned upside-down, Grandfather. I need your advice."

"Do you?" Grandfather plopped back onto the settee, smile in place. "Why come to me, lass? Not your mum?"

"Because when things are topsy-turvy, you seem to know what to do."

"True. But so do you."

Jane shivered. "No, I do not. I was perfectly happy with my life as it was. Then John began to change, and Captain Ingram—"

"A fine young man is Ingram," Grandfather said brightly. "My advice is to run off with him. You like kissing him well enough."

Jane's face flamed. "Grandfather!"

"I do not know why you are so ashamed. I saw you kissing him in the garden, and young Thomas says you kissed him at the bonfire." Grandfather shook his head in impatience. "Latch on to him, Janie, and kiss him for life."

Jane's face grew hotter, her mortification complete. "You ought to have made yourself known instead of lurking in the shrubbery."

"Tut, girl. I was out for a walk, a good stride through the yew hedges. Not lurking anywhere. You were standing plain as day by those ridiculous statues. Which is why I don't understand your shame. You did not kick Ingram in the dangles and run away. You embraced him. With enthusiasm."

"Even so." Jane's embarrassment warred with elation as she thought of the kiss. "I cannot disappoint my family and uproot my life on a whim."

"Why not?"

"Because …" Jane waved her hands. "What a fool I'd be. I barely know Captain Ingram. He might be the basest scoundrel on land, ready to abandon me at a moment's notice. The real world is not a fairy tale, Grandfather."

"Thank heavens for that. Fairy tales are horrible — the fae ain't the nice little people painted in books for maiden ladies. Trust me. I'm descended from witches, and I know all about the fae."

"Of course, Grandfather." If not stopped, Grandfather could go on for some time about how Shakespeare based Macbeth's witches on the women in his mother's family. "What I mean is I can't simply change everything because a handsome gentleman kissed me," she said.

"You can, you know. This is why you came to me for advice, young lady, and not your mum. Isobel is my pride and joy, she is, but she's the practical sort. The airiness of your grandmother and the wickedness of my side of the family didn't manifest in her. Isobel's more like me dad, a stolid Scotsman who never put a foot wrong in his life. Didn't stop the Hanoverians taking all he had." Grandfather's gaze held the remote rage of long ago, then he shook his head and refocused on the present.

"Janie, you are unhappy because you believe life should be simple. You long for it to be. You fancied yourself willing to marry Barnett because it was the easy choice. He's familiar to your family, you know what to expect from him, and you'd congratulated yourself for not having to chase down a husband to look after you the rest of your life. But you'd be disappointed in him. He might be the simplest choice for a husband, but you'd end up looking after *him*, and you know it."

"Why is such a thing so bad?" Jane asked, heart heavy. "Grandmother looked after *you*."

Grandfather shook his head. "She and I looked after each other. And we did not have a peaceful life at first—our families were furious with us, and we had to weather that, and find a way to live, *and* raise our children. It weren't no easy matter, my girl, but that is the point. Life is complicated. It's hard, hard work. So many try to find a path around that, but though that path might look clear, it can be full of misery. You sit helplessly while things happen around you instead of grabbing your life by the horns and shaking it about. Happiness is worth the trouble, the difficult choices, the path full of brambles. Do not sit and let things flow by you, Jane. You deserve much more than that. Take your happiness, my love. Do not let this moment pass."

Jane sat silently. She felt limp, drained—had since she'd told John they could never be married. She thought she'd feel freedom once she'd been truthful with John, as Spencer had told her she would, but at present, Jane only wanted to curl up and weep.

"But I could misstep," she said. "I could charge down the difficult path and take a brutal tumble."

"That you could. And then you rise up and try again. Or you could huddle by the wayside and let happiness slip past. If you don't grab joy while you can, you might not have another chance."

Jane's heart began to beat more strongly. "I am a

woman. I must be prudent. A man who falls can be helped up by his friends. A woman who falls is ostracized by hers."

Grandfather shook his head. "Only if those friends are scoundrels. I imagine your family would stand by you no matter what happened. I know *I* would." He raised his hands, palms facing her. "But you are worrying because you've been taught to worry. Do you truly believe Ingram is a hardened roué? With a string of broken hearts and ruined women behind him? We'd have heard about such things. Barnett would have told us—you know how much he loves to gossip. And he wouldn't have brought Captain Ingram home to you and your mum and dad if he thought the man a bad 'un, would he?"

Jane had to concede. "I suppose not …"

"Your dad knows everyone in England, and he's no fool. He'd have heard of Ingram's reputation if the man had a foul one, and he'd have never let him inside. It's harder than you'd think to be a secret rake in this country. *Someone* will know, and feel no remorse spreading the tale."

Jane didn't answer. Everything Grandfather said was reasonable. Still, she'd seen what happened when a woman married badly—she found herself saddled with an insipid, feckless man who did nothing but disgrace his family and distress his friends.

The man John could so easily become …

"Spencer Ingram seems a fine enough lad to me," Grandfather went on. "Family's respectable too, from what I hear. Besides, Ingram is a good Scottish name."

"Of course." Jane gave a shaky laugh. "That is why you like him."

"One of the reasons. There are many others." Grandfather jumped to his feet. "What are you waiting for, Janie? Your happiness walked in the door last night. Go to it—go to *him*."

"I don't regret telling John I will never marry him," Jane said with conviction. "And I suppose you're right. I won't send Captain Ingram away, or push him aside because I'm mortified. He will be visiting a while longer. We can get to know each other, and perhaps …"

Her words faded as Grandfather snorted. "*Get to know each other? Perhaps?* Have you heard nothing I've said?" His eyes flashed. "You are trying to make things comfortable again, which means pushing aside decisions, waiting for things to transpire instead of forcing them to."

He pointed imperiously at the door. "Out you go, Jane. Now. Find Captain Ingram. Tell him you will marry him. No thinking it over, or lying awake pondering choices, or waiting to see what happens. Go to him this instant."

Jane rose, her heart pounding. "I can't tell him I'll marry him, Grandfather. He hasn't asked me."

"Then ask *him*. Your grandmother did me. She tired of me shillyshallying. So she stepped up and told me I either married her, or she walked away and looked for someone else."

Jane covered her fears with a laugh. She could picture Maggie MacDonald doing just that. "But I am not Grandmother."

Grandfather's eyes softened. "Oh, yes, you are. You are so like her, Janie, you don't realize. Her spitting image when she was young, and you have her spirit. She knew it too." Tears beaded on his lashes. "I miss her so."

"Oh, Grandfather." Janie launched herself at him, enfolding him into her arms. Grandfather rested his head on her shoulder, a fragile old man, his bones too light.

After a time, they pushed away from each other, both trying to smile.

"Go to him, Janie," Grandfather said. "For her sake."

Jane kissed his faded cheek and spun for the door. As she turned to close it behind her, she saw Grandfather's tears flow unchecked down his face, he wiping them away with a fold of his plaid.

CHAPTER 6

*S*pencer observed that Barnett did not seem too morose that Lady Jane had thrown him over. He watched Barnett fling himself into the hunt, crowing over the things he'd found for his group, all the while glancing raptly at the daughter of guests from Kent. His behavior was not so much of a man bereaved as one reprieved.

Spencer knew that if Jane had given *him* the push, he'd be miserable, tearing at his hair and beating his breast like the best operatic hero.

He feared Jane had dismissal in mind when she gazed down from the upper gallery and caught his eye. She gave him a long look before she skimmed down the stairs and disappeared into the library.

Spencer, who'd found none of the items on his list, his heart not in the game, handed his paper to Thomas and told the lad to carry on.

"Jane?" Spencer whispered as he entered the library. It was dark, a few candles burning for the sake of the gamers, the fire half-hearted against the cold. The chill was why no one lingered here—the room was quite empty.

Spencer shut the door. "Jane?"

She turned from the shadows beside the fireplace. Spencer approached her, one reluctant pace at a time.

When he was a few strides away, Jane smiled at him. That smile blazed like sunshine, lighting the room to its darkest corners.

"Captain Ingram," Lady Jane said. "Will you marry me?"

Spencer ceased breathing. He knew his heart continued to beat, because it pounded blood through him in hot washes. But he felt nothing, as though he'd been wound in bandages, like the time a French saber had pierced his shoulder and the surgeon had swaddled his upper body like a babe's.

That shoulder throbbed, the old pain resurfacing, and Spencer's breath rushed back into his lungs.

"Jane …"

"I am sincere, I assure you," Jane said, as though she supposed he'd argue with her. "I know I am doing this topsy-turvy, but—"

Spencer laid shaking hands on her shoulders, the blue silk of her gown warmed by her body. "Which is the right way 'round for you, my beautiful, beautiful fae."

"Grandfather would faint if he heard you say so," Jane said with merriment. "I believe he's rather afraid of the fae. Even if he married one."

Spencer tightened his clasp on her. He never remembered how Jane ended up in his arms, but in the next instant he was kissing her, deeply, possessively, and she responded with the mad passion he'd seen in her eyes.

That kiss ended, but they scarcely had time to draw a breath before the next kiss began. And the next.

They ended up in the wing chair that reposed before the fire, placed so a reader might keep his or her feet warm. Spencer's large frame took up most of it, but there was room for Jane on his lap.

They kissed again, Spencer cradling her.

How much time sped by, Spencer had no idea, but at last he drew Jane to rest on his shoulder.

"Shall we adjourn to Gretna Green?" he asked in a low voice.

Jane raised her head, her blue eyes bright in the darkened room. "No, indeed. I wish my family and friends to be present. But soon."

"How fortunate that my leave is for a month. Time enough to have the banns read in your parish church. And then what? Follow me and the drum? It can be a hard life."

Jane brushed his cheek. "I do want to go with you. I am willing to face the challenge, to forsake the safer path." She spoke the words forcefully, as though waiting for Spencer to dissuade her.

He had no intention of it. With Jane by his side, camp life would cease to be bleak. "I plan to sell my commission a few years from now, in any case. I do not see myself as a career army man, though I am fond of travel."

"I long to travel."

The words were adamant. With Jane's restlessness and fire, Spencer believed her. "After that, I will have a house waiting for me," he said. "One of my father's minor estates."

Her smile beamed. "Excellent."

"Not really—it needs much work. Again, I am not promising you softness."

"I do not want it." Jane kissed his chin. "I am resilient. And resourceful. I like to be doing things, and I do not mean embroidery. Come to think of it, my grandmother never did embroidery in her life."

"I know." Spencer nuzzled her hair. "Your grandfather spoke much about her when I met him in London."

Jane stilled. Very slowly, she lifted her head. "You met my grandfather in London?"

Spencer nodded. "Last spring. I was on another leave-taking, much shorter, to visit my family. I spent a night in London, and at the tavern near my lodgings, I met an amusing old Scotsman who was pleased to sit up with me telling stories. I mentioned my friendship with Barnett, and your grandfather was delighted."

"He was, was he?" Jane's tone turned ominous.

"Indeed. But when I arrived last night, he asked me not to speak of our previous meeting to anyone. I have no idea why, but I saw no reason not to indulge him."

He leaned to kiss her again, to enjoy the taste of her fire, but Jane put her hand on his chest.

"Will you excuse me for one moment, Spencer?"

Spencer skimmed his fingertips across her cheek. "When you speak my name, I cannot refuse you, love."

Her eyes softened, but she scrambled from his lap. Spencer rose with her, a steadying hand on her waist. "I won't be long," she promised.

Jane strode from the room, her head high. Spencer

watched her go, then chuckled to himself and followed her.

~

"Grandfather."

She found he'd moved to a smaller, warmer sitting room, only this time he'd truly nodded off. The old man jumped awake and then to his feet, the whisky flask he'd been holding clanging to the floor.

"What the devil? Janie, what is it?"

Jane pointed an accusing finger at his face. "You met Captain Ingram in London this past spring."

"Did I?" Grandfather frowned, then stroked his jaw in contemplation. "Now that you call it to my mind, I believe I did. My memory ain't what it used to be."

"I cry foul." Jane planted her hands on her hips. "You knew he was John's friend. *You* put the idea into John's head to bring Captain Ingram here for Hogmanay, didn't you? Do not prevaricate with me, please."

"Hmm. I might have mentioned our meeting in a letter to young Barnett."

"And you told John to send Captain Ingram into the house first."

"Well, he is dark-haired. And tall. And what ladies believe is handsome." Grandfather spread his hands. "My prediction came true, you see? You will marry this year's First-Footer. I see by your blush that he has accepted your proposal."

Jane's cheeks indeed were hot. "Prediction, my eye. You planned this from the beginning, you old fraud."

Grandfather drew himself up. "And if I did? And if I met Ingram's family and determined that they were worthy of you? Captain Ingram is a far better match for you than Barnett. My lady ancestors were witches, yes, but they always had contingencies to make certain the spell worked."

Deep, rumbling laughter made Jane spin around. Spencer leaned on the doorframe, gray eyes sparkling in mirth.

"Bless you that you did," he said. He came to Jane and put a strong hand on her arm. "You and your ancestors will always have my gratitude, sir. Jane and I will be married by the end of the month."

Grandfather gave Jane a hopeful look. "All's well, that end's well?"

Jane dashed forward in a burst of love and caught her grandfather in an exuberant embrace. "Yes, Grandfather. Thank you. Thank you. I love you so much."

"Go on with you now." Grandfather struggled away, but the tears in his eyes touched her heart. "The pair of ye, be off. Ye have much more kissing to do. It's Hogmanay still."

Spencer twined his hand through Jane's. "An excellent suggestion."

"And don't either of you worry about Barnett. I've already caught him kissing Miss Pembroke."

Jane blinked. Miss Pembroke was the daughter of her parents' friends from Kent. "He is quick off the mark. The wretch."

"Then he can toast us at our wedding," Spencer said. He pulled Jane firmly to the door. "I believe I'd like to adjourn to the library again, to continue our … planning."

Jane melted to him, her anger and exasperation dissolving. She needed this man, who'd come to her so unexpectedly to lift her out of her dreary life. "A fine idea."

In the cool of the hall, Spencer bent to Jane and whispered in her ear. "You are beauty and light. I love you, Janie. This I already know."

"I already know I love you too."

They sealed their declaration with a kiss that burned with a wildness Jane had been longing for, the fierce freedom of her youth released once more.

~

Left alone in the sitting room, Hamish MacDonald raised his flask to the painting of a beautiful woman whose flowing hair spilled from under a wide-brimmed hat. She smiled at him over a basket of flowers, her bodice sliding to bare one seductive shoulder. Her eyes were deep blue, her hair black as night.

"I did it, Maggie," he said, his voice scratchy. "I've seen to it that our girl will be happy. Bless you, love."

He toasted the portrait, done by the great Ramsay, and drank deeply of malt whisky.

He swore that Maggie, his beloved wife, heart of his heart, forever in his thoughts, winked at him.

~

Thank you for reading! If you enjoy Regencies, see *Duke in Search of a Duchess,* in which the Duke of Ashford never dreams his children will recruit the busybody young widow next door to help him find a new wife.

FIONA AND THE THREE WISE HIGHLANDERS

A MACKENZIES / MCBRIDES HOLIDAY NOVELLA

CHAPTER 1

Kilmorgan Castle, 1892

"Papa."

Ian Mackenzie, at his desk in the attic room he'd turned into his private study, warmed as he heard the voice of his youngest daughter, Megan. He looked up from a letter he'd been transcribing, one from the 1350s that described his ancestor, Old Dan Mackenzie, and his feats at the Battle of Berwick. All thoughts of the past, the battle for Scotland, and Old Dan's reward of a dukedom, fled.

Megan was ten, with the glossy brown hair and blue eyes of her mother. She loved books and music, happy to sit reading or playing sweet notes on the piano. She was also as interested in the family's history as Ian.

Ian said nothing, waiting for Megan to tell him why she'd come. She was shy, as he was, but she spoke up firmly when she had something to say.

"What happened to Stuart Cameron, Papa?" Megan

crossed the room to stand beside his desk. She had a bow in her hair, a blue one to match her eyes, and it rose above her head like fairy's wings. Ian had the sudden impression that she *was* a fairy, and she'd fly away from him if he weren't careful.

"Papa?"

Ian forced his gaze from the bow and settled it on her eyes. "Aye, lass. Stuart Cameron. Will Mackenzie's best mate."

A few days ago, Ian had regaled the younger Mackenzie generation with the tale of Alec Mackenzie, brother to their ancestor who'd survived the Battle of Culloden. Alec had rescued the family friend, Stuart Cameron, from captivity and certain death.

Ian carefully folded his papers and pushed them aside. Old Dan would have to wait. He lifted his daughter to his lap, his arm around her waist to hold her steady.

"Stuart Cameron traveled to France with Alec and Will after escaping from prison," Ian began without inflection. "He returned to Scotland in December of 1746, where he met Fiona Macdonald—"

"No, Papa." Megan gazed up at him reproachfully. "That is not how you begin a story."

Ian felt a trickle of mirth. His family believed him a stickler for procedure, but whenever he deviated from it, *they* grew bewildered and guided him back.

"Aye, 'tis so." Ian held Megan closer. "I will start again."

He leaned back in the chair and closed his eyes, bringing to mind the exact words of the letters he'd read, plus the diary of Fiona Macdonald, great-great-

great-great aunt by marriage to his mother, Elspeth Cameron.

"Once upon a time …"

~

Near Inverness, December, 1746

THE THREE MEN WHO SWAGGERED INTO BALTHAZAR'S inn were bundled in drab thick coats, boots that must have squelched through every patch of mud from here to Aberdeen, drenched hats pulled down to their ears.

Fiona Macdonald sat very still in the warm corner near the fireplace, feet buried in the straw on the floor. Beside her, Una, her maid, long-time companion, and fellow conspirator, stiffened, ready to become a guard dog in an instant. Una was not happy that Fiona had to rest in the common room, but the inn was crowded tonight, and a chamber was being readied for her by the innkeeper's daughter.

"We come bearing gifts," the smallest of the men sang out. He was a disreputable fellow, who removed his hat to reveal sun-bleached brown hair. His skin had the tough brown hue of old leather, but his smile was wide, his teeth whole if stained. "Is that not what ye do when ye see a star guiding ye to an inn at Christmastide? Is there a wee babe in the stables we should visit?"

The men in the smoky common room laughed. Through the din, the innkeeper, Balthazar, stroked his beard with his fingers. "There's already one wise man here, Gair Murray, and I'd not let ye within ten feet of a wee babe."

"Ye know me, then?" Gair's smile widened. "And ye bandy me name about, do ye? Worth a free jar, I'm thinking."

"Everyone knows ye, Gair. You're among friends here."

Not likely, Fiona thought as she wrapped her hands around her cooling mug of tea. Gair Murray, a smuggler, had no true friends, not really. He did favors for men up and down Scotland, but for pay, at the same time on the lookout for anything he could lift for himself.

His only friend in the world, if he could be called so, was the thin but much taller man next to him. Padruig looked out at the world with one gray eye, the other, lost in some long-ago battle, covered with a leather patch.

Both men wore cloaks over their coats, Padruig's black, Gair's brown with a stripe that made it appear suspiciously like an old tartan. Fiona hoped he wouldn't be caught wearing a forbidden plaid.

Padruig, as usual, said nothing as the more garrulous Gair bantered with the innkeeper.

Fiona regarded the third figure with growing tension. He was a huge bear of a man, a Highlander without doubt, his hair a strange shade of black. Soot, she realized as a streak of it came off when he removed his hat. He was trying to disguise the true color.

He was muffled to his ears in a plain gray scarf, he the only of the three not to have a cloak wrapped about him. He hunched his back as though trying to conceal his height, but he did a poor job of it. This was a man used to standing straight, proud, arrogant.

Perhaps his spirit had been broken, as so many of

them had been. Fiona had once been a proud Highlander herself.

And still am. We are defeated, not gone.

The man had to pull down his scarf to drink the tankard of ale Balthazar shoved onto a table for the three men. More soot smeared from his hair, which shone like a streak of sudden flame.

Only one man had hair that brilliant shade of red. But he was dead, captured by the Hanoverians after Culloden, taken prisoner, vanished. Fiona's heart had died that day. He'd have been executed by now. Fiona's nightmares had showed her his death so many times in the last eight months that she was certain of it.

Until the man turned his head and looked at her.

Blue eyes like summer skies skewered her, and the firm mouth that had once kissed like fire pinched into a frown. He rose from the stool he'd just taken, as though unable to stop himself.

Stuart Cameron.

Her brother's enemy and the man who'd stolen her peace before he'd run off to join the doomed army of *Teàrlach mhic Seamas*.

~

PADRUIG EYED STUART IN CONCERN, THOUGH GAIR continued telling the men next to them some tale he was inventing about their travels. Gair's constant banter kept people mollified until too late to recognize his perfidy.

Fiona Macdonald shouldn't be sitting in a wayside tavern in the middle of the Scottish Highlands with English soldiers hunting down any they even thought smelled like a Jacobite. She should have taken ship months ago to France or the Low Countries, or at least be home with her brother, anywhere she'd be safe. It was typical of her to decide not to flee or hide.

Stuart could not stop himself crossing the tavern to her. The room was crowded, so much so that none paid much attention to another weary traveler pushing through their midst.

The eagle-eyed maid, Una, glared up at Stuart as he approached. So she was still with Fiona. Loyal of her. Fiona sipped tea as though she noticed no one.

Stuart knew Fiona had seen him and recognized him. Best to corner her before she burst out with his true identity ... not that the Fiona Macdonald he knew would do such a thing, although she might in her surprise. Or Una might, indignant at his return.

Stuart came to a halt next to Fiona, pretending to warm his hands at the fire. His heart thumped with Fiona's nearness, the fire nothing to the slow heat that churned through his body.

It had been so long since he'd seen her, touched her, simply enjoyed her presence. He'd dreamed of her, the image of her face, her smile keeping him from the very bottom of despair.

"What are ye doing here, lass?" Stuart asked in a quiet voice.

"What are you?" Fiona's answer came as quietly. She rested her mug on her lap. "You're alive, I see."

"Aye. Barely."

"What happened to ye?"

"A guest of his majesty." Stuart shrugged, trying to

maintain the stance of a servant who mooched along after Gair and Padruig. "Then France."

Fiona's eyes widened slightly. She had the loveliest eyes, green like jade in sunlight, which set off her very dark hair. He saw her realization that he'd been a prisoner—and she'd never know all of that horror if Stuart could help it. Escaped by the skin of his teeth—and with the help of the Mackenzie brothers—over the Channel to France. He'd rested and recovered there, but he'd soon longed to be back in Scotland, and so had hunted up the expert smugglers Gair and Padruig, and hired them to provide him passage.

"Ye should have stayed." Fiona's voice was barely above a whisper.

Did she mean in Paris or prison? Stuart let the corner of his mouth pull into a half smile. "Missing home."

"Home isn't safe."

"Is it safe for you?" Stuart countered.

He saw the flinch Fiona tried to hide, though Una didn't bother to smother her scowl. Not much older than Fiona, Una had the flaxen hair of a Viking and the demeanor to match. She guarded Fiona like a lioness. For that, Stuart would forgive her scowls.

"Safe enough," Fiona said. "The soldiers don't always stop a woman."

"More fool they." The greatest fault the Hanoverians had was to underestimate Scotswomen. The English kept their own women so sheltered and subdued they assumed their northern neighbors did the same. "I thought ye'd be on a ship heading across the seas." *Without your waste of a brother,* he finished silently.

"Broc is ill," Fiona said, the gleam in her eyes telling Stuart she knew what he was thinking. "He never recovered after his injury at Falkirk."

"Does he still claim it was me who shot him?" Stuart allowed the smile to form.

Broc Macdonald, who'd stubbornly thrown in his lot with King Geordie, had suffered a leg wound at the Battle of Falkirk and had been carried, wailing, from the field. So Stuart had been told. He hadn't witnessed the injury.

"Yes." Fiona's own smile flashed then vanished. "Though I told him ye couldn't have."

"Loyal woman."

"'Tisn't loyalty. I know the truth."

Stuart barely heard her. Fiona's smile transcended her drab garments, shawl, and the faded cap she wore under a broad-brimmed hat. The ensemble made her look like an ordinary farm woman, instead of the laird's sister she was. Her beauty was like a breath of air in this musty place, returning the memory of her laughter, her quick wit, her sparkling eyes.

He recalled dancing with her in her brother's house not long before Prince Teàrlach marched on Edinburgh, her warm hand in his, her lithe grace as they moved in the patterns of the reel.

He recalled her red lips that neared his as they turned, hand in hand, then moved tantalizingly out of reach. The kiss on the terrace after that, when he'd wrapped his plaid around her and warmed them both.

"Still," Stuart made himself say, "kind of ye to put in a word for me."

"You didn't shoot him because you were keeping

Duncan Mackenzie alive." Fiona's sudden frown almost matched Una's in severity. She hadn't liked Duncan's recklessness and had feared he'd be Stuart's death. Duncan had perished on Culloden Moor, the poor bastard. He'd had all the arrogance but not the quick thinking of his younger brothers.

"For my sins." Stuart leaned closer, returning to the pretense of warming his hands. "But what are ye doing *here*, lass? In the middle of nowhere the day before Christmas Eve?"

Fiona glanced behind Stuart and folded her lips. *Hmm*. She didn't want to say in front of anyone who might hear. He saw none but Highlanders in the room, but one couldn't be certain which way any man's loyalty lay.

If she were any other lady, Stuart would shrug and not pursue it. But this was Fiona Macdonald, and she never did anything not worth learning about. He'd have the secret out of her. Perhaps later, in a dark chamber, with the door locked …

A distinct presence made itself felt—or smelled—at his side. Both women winced, and even Stuart took a step away. Gair rarely bathed, and the heat of the close room made him ripe.

"The question I ought to ask," Fiona said, pretending to ignore Gair. "Is why are you in such disreputable company?"

"Ah, she breaks me heart," Gair said with a dry chuckle. "We're saving his life, lass, is the answer. Spiriting him across the land to his home."

"Spiriting?" Una wrinkled her nose. "Ye couldn't

spirit anything but whisky, Gair Murray. From the smell of things, ye've had a lot of it."

Gair laughed without malice. One thing Stuart liked about the man was that he knew exactly who he was and had no aspiration to be anything else.

"A fine reunion ye're having," Gair said. "But it's time to pay the piper. Not that I play the pipes. Can't abide the things."

Stuart straightened in puzzlement. "I paid ye, Gair. In advance. Every bit of silver I had. Ye insisted, I remember." He still felt the sting of handing over the last coins he had in his sporran. He hoped the king's armies hadn't stolen the rest of what he'd stashed at home.

"Aye." Gair returned the look without shame. "That was *my* payment. Now for Padruig."

Bloody man. Stuart had always known he couldn't trust Gair. To smuggle Stuart into Scotland and across the country without betraying him, yes. With his money? No.

"Ye don't share your take with Padruig?" Stuart asked, as though surprised. "I'd reconsider, Gair. He's a dangerous man."

He and Gair glanced as one at Padruig. The man leaned his left elbow on the table near a large tankard of ale, while he amused himself twirling a dagger in his right hand. His lank and long hair, worn leather eyepatch, and the concentration in his good eye did not lend reassurance.

Gair's humor didn't fade. "Oh, he's happy with what I give him. This is something special, he tells me."

The innkeeper had vanished, tending to whatever innkeepers tend to, but the common room remained crowded. A few lads ran about serving the loud Highlanders, while the window grew dark with the cold midwinter night.

Stuart smothered a sigh and gave Fiona and Una a truncated bow. "Excuse me, ladies."

Gair guffawed and followed Stuart across the room to the table. Padruig flipped the blade through competent fingers and let it land, point down, buried a half inch into the wood.

"The landlord won't be happy with that," Stuart remarked as he slid onto a stool.

Padruig said nothing. Where Gair could talk the hind leg off a mule, Padruig was silence itself.

"What do you want?" Stuart asked him. "I'll have no more money until I reach home, and even then I might have nothing. The bloody English will have confiscated everything." Possibly not the cache of jewels he'd hidden well before he'd left to join the Jacobite army, but Stuart wasn't fool enough to mention jewels in front of Gair. "Take your share out of Gair's hide."

Gair went off into gales of hilarity, but Padruig's face remained impassive.

"'Tis nae coin I want."

Padruig so rarely spoke, that when he did, he drew attention. Even Gair ceased his laughter. Padruig opened the tankard and took a loud sip of ale.

"What then?" Stuart asked impatiently.

Padruig sipped again, set down the tankard, and wiped his mouth on his sleeve.

"A *sgian dubh*."

Stuart's brows climbed. "A knife? Is that all? Cumberland's men might have taken all of those from my home as well, but likely I can find one stashed somewhere."

"No." Padruig's harsh word dried up Stuart's relief. "One particular *sgian dubh*, lost at Culloden Moor. Bring me that, and your debt to me will be paid."

CHAPTER 2

Fiona neared Stuart's table in time to hear Padruig's words. She ought to have remained quietly in the corner—Una hissed for her to remember what they were there for—but Fiona was drawn to Stuart like an arrow to its mark.

Even hunched into his coat, his hat restored over his awful hair, he held a power that filled the room. Fiona could no more keep from him than she could cease breathing.

"Oh, aye?" Stuart demanded as Padruig studied him. "Ye wish me te crawl about on me belly in the grass at Culloden, pushing aside the bones to look for an eating knife?"

"Perhaps it is special to him." Fiona slid onto a stool next to Stuart's.

Stuart jumped, but Gair and Padruig, who'd seen her come, accepted her without comment.

"'Tis." Padruig nodded at Fiona.

Gair shrugged. "First he's told me of it. But if he

wants a *sgian dubh*, I suggest ye find it for him," he said pointedly to Stuart. "He won't let you loose from the bargain without it."

"Then I never will be," Stuart growled. "What ye want is bloody impossible."

The anguish in Stuart's voice as he talked about searching Culloden Moor was similar to what she'd heard in other Highlanders she'd spoken to since that battle. They'd seen horror, and while they'd survived, they'd never completely recover from it.

"Not necessarily." Fiona set her mostly empty tea mug on the table. "The innkeeper's daughter has collected things from the moor and keeps them in a room here. She calls it her Chamber of Sorrows. Perhaps she's found your *sgian dubh*."

Stuart's blue eyes skewered her. Fiona wished she still held her mug so she could hide behind it. Stuart gazed straight into her soul.

She hadn't quite adjusted to the fact that he'd returned. Alive. Part of her was in shock, believing him a ghost who'd vanish as soon as she touched him. The other part sang in heavenly thanks, that Stuart had escaped and was whole. A quarter of an hour ago she'd been mourning him. Now he was here, and joy was burgeoning. When the shock faded, she'd be giddy and incoherent.

What they'd be to each other after a year apart, if anything at all, remained to be seen, but for the moment, it was enough that Stuart was here.

Now he continued to stare at her as though he had no idea what she was talking about.

"Oh, aye?" Gair answered her.

"I'll ask her if you can look," Fiona offered. "She's an agreeable young woman, I'm finding. Though be careful, Gair. She has made no secret of the fact that she'd like a husband."

Gair burst out laughing, which had the unfortunate consequence of him spitting droplets of ale across the table. "No fear on that score, lass. Gair's not the marrying kind."

Fiona had spoken in jest. Carrie, the innkeeper's daughter, had made it known she'd prefer an Englishman who could take her to softer living, so Gair was safe, but she did not explain. None of the three men at this table would have any use for Englishmen at the moment, even theoretical ones.

"You do that, *chaileag*." Gair took another slurp of ale. "Padruig will be grateful. I imagine this one will be too." He jerked his thumb at Stuart, carefully not calling him by name.

Fiona said nothing about Gair addressing her as *girl*, or of him using the forbidden Erse tongue. It was not easy to cease conversing in a language you'd spoken all the days of your life.

Stuart kept his gaze on Fiona. Unnerving, that. She longed to ask him what had happened to him, how he'd escaped, how he'd survived. And to tell him what she'd been doing since the day last year when they'd parted so stormily at her brother's house. She'd been travelling the Highlands too, though she'd returned home from time to time to rest and plan. But she'd tried to stay away from her brother as often as and for as long as she could. Handy to know so many women in the Highlands with sentiments similar to hers.

They couldn't discuss such things, though, not here, in a tavern any traveler might enter.

I missed you, Stuart. I feared for you, my heart.

Fiona lifted her tea mug and drank the last bitter dregs, but she couldn't avoid Stuart's scrutiny.

∽

STUART FOLLOWED FIONA INTO THE CHAMBER OF Sorrows located in the rear of the inn — Fiona had somehow persuaded the landlord's daughter to admit them. Though Stuart hadn't heard what Fiona had said to Carrie when the young woman had returned to the taproom, he wasn't surprised Fiona had arranged it. She had a way with her, did Fiona Macdonald.

When she'd said *sgian dubh*, the words soft on her tongue, Stuart's entire body had become incandescent.

Fiona was a true lady of the Highlands, her speech holding the unmistakable lilt. Far gentler than the harsh voices of the men he'd been surrounded by, her consonants almost a whisper against the liquid vowels.

Stuart had missed her until he ached. He hadn't realized how much until he'd been trussed up in that dark building in the farmlands of southern England, unsure whether he'd live or die. The thought of never seeing Fiona again had been almost as bad as the creative torture the English bastards had inflicted on him.

To find Fiona here, in this wayward place, far too close to the field where so many of his friends and family had perished was … odd. Why was she here? Fiona never did anything without a reason, and Stuart would have to pry out of her what that reason was.

The chamber was filled with sorrows indeed. Swords and pistols hung on the walls, and tables and boxes held knives, buckles, and other smaller relics. So much. A testament to the many who'd fallen.

Stuart halted just inside the door as the noise and stench of the battle suddenly poured back to him. The crack of gunfire, the acrid smell of powder, the screams of the dying, the blood-pounding rage that had kept Stuart fighting, followed by the intense grief of watching Duncan Mackenzie fall, his brothers and father swallowed by the smoke.

Gair pushed past as Stuart froze on the threshold, unable to move.

Fiona was already following the red-haired Carrie through the room, gazing at the assortment, her footfalls hushed.

Gair, who'd raided battlefields, beached ships, burned-out houses, and the like, had no qualms about examining the collection. He kept his hands behind his back much of the time, as though vowing he'd not filch anything, though Stuart noticed Fiona keeping a close eye on him.

"'Tis not here," Padruig announced after he and Gair had scanned the room for about half an hour. Carrie remained in the corner, letting them look but making certain they didn't nick anything.

As far as Stuart could tell, Padruig hadn't done much searching—Gair and Fiona had picked through boxes and studied objects on the shelves.

"Plenty of knives, though." Gair gestured at a case full of them. "Ye could find a good one. I'm sure the lass would give it to ye for a fair price."

Padruig, more stoic than usual, shook his head. He turned his back on Gair, pressed past Stuart, and made his way through the outer chambers to the noisy taproom.

Gair shrugged and began to follow. Fiona hurried to the door to stand beside Stuart and block Gair's path.

"Put them back," Fiona said evenly.

Gair gave her an innocent stare. "What are you on about, lass?"

Gair was a small man, and Fiona could look him straight in the eye. "Please." The word was firm, no pleading in it.

Gair's cheeks stained red. He heaved a sigh, sent Stuart an aggrieved glance, and pulled three buckles, a knife, a ring, and a few coins from his pockets. As the innkeeper's daughter watched, hands on hips, Gair returned them to the last basket he'd been sorting through.

Astonishing. Stuart hadn't seen him pocket anything, the sly sod.

"Is that all?" Fiona asked.

Gair let out another sigh and dropped two more coins into the basket. He lifted his hands. "That is all. Sorry, lass." He flashed Carrie a grin and slid past Stuart and out.

Stuart still couldn't move. The sorrow in the room pressed at him like a wave of chill fog until he could barely breathe.

Fiona laid her hand on his arm. Her touch, the warm pressure of her fingers, cut through the coldness, and the air began to clear. Stuart's feet came unstuck. He drew a long breath and stepped aside, giving Fiona room to leave the chamber.

Her hand slid from his coat, her face turned up to his, her green eyes searching. Stuart swallowed, suppressing the sharp need to enfold her in his arms and crush her to him. He remained still, which took all his strength. Fiona at last ducked around him, her expression unreadable.

Carrie remained, not offering to see them out. When Stuart glanced back, he saw her straightening the things Gair had displaced, her movements gentle.

Stuart caught up to Fiona and grasped her elbow, intending to take her aside where they could speak alone, but a maid hurried to her and said, "Chamber's ready, milady."

Of course, Fiona would want to trade the smoky and crowded outer room for privacy and relative comfort. She thanked the maid and started to follow her.

"Fio—" Stuart stopped himself as the maid gave him and then Fiona a curious stare. "Miss Macdonald."

"Thank you for your assistance, sir," Fiona said, maintaining her serenity. "Good night."

Damn and blast. Stuart could only bow like a good servant. He watched as she disappeared into one of the large chambers they'd just walked past to reach the collection. Una, with a severe scowl, shut the door.

Stuart glared at the blank wood for a few moments then gave up and returned to the taproom, remembering to shuffle like a lackey.

A harried maid slammed fresh tankards in front of Gair and Padruig as Stuart resumed his seat. Stuart had not had a chance to drink his first tankard, but Gair and Padruig were experts at putting away ale.

"Macdonald," Padruig said.

Stuart took a fortifying sip. The ale wasn't bad, as far as ale went, though he'd had better. "What Macdonald?"

"The lass's brother."

Stuart had thought that was who he meant. "Broc. A complete arse. Stay away from him."

Over my dead body will my sister run off with a Cameron and a rebel! Broc had shouted it at the top of his voice, and Fiona had quietly told Stuart he'd better go.

Broc Macdonald had inherited his father's lands, becoming laird of the surrounding glen. He had an ancient castle that had been made comfortable with modern furniture and carpets. So why was Fiona not there, warm and snug, even if she'd have to look after the ungrateful swine, and instead out in the deep cold between Inverness and Culloden Moor?

"He has it."

Stuart snapped back to Padruig. Even Gair ceased his drinking to frown at his partner. "Who has what?" Gair demanded.

"Broc Macdonald has the *sgian dubh*."

"Oh, aye? We just spent half an hour picking through that dross, and ye tell me it's for nothing?"

Stuart eyed Gair calmly. "You only think it a waste because Fiona caught you nicking half of it. Why do you think he has your knife, Padruig?"

"Worth a chance, wasn't it?" Padruig said. "The young Macdonald lass put me in mind of her brother. He happily watched his kinsmen be slaughtered then picked them clean. I saw him doing it." Padruig folded his thin lips together, having made the longest speech Stuart had ever heard him utter.

Stuart hadn't been aware Padruig and Gair had been anywhere near Culloden during the battle, but he said nothing about that. They'd been on hand to help the surviving Mackenzies flee to France in Gair's rickety ship, true, but he hadn't realized they'd come in from shore.

"What are ye saying?" Gair asked Padruig. "Ye want the lass to go home and tell her brother to give it up to ye?"

"I'm saying *he* should." Padruig flicked a bony forefinger at Stuart. He lifted his tankard. "And we should go along with them."

Gair regarded his partner in amazement. "When did ye become so daft? It's Christmas in a few days, and I planned to put me feet up here and wait for Hogmanay."

Stuart lifted his hand for attention. "What makes you think Broc Macdonald will even let me near his house?"

"Ye have his sister," Padruig said.

Stuart shook his head. "I haven't seen the woman in more than a year. That's nae *having* her, Padruig."

Padruig shrugged as though that was something Stuart needed to work out.

"I agree with Gair," Stuart said. "You've run mad. I've never heard ye once mention the name of Fiona's brother or this *sgian dubh* ye want."

"The lass brought it to mind."

So calm was Padruig, as though what he asked was a trifle Stuart could fetch for him in five minutes.

"Help me understand." Stuart tried to keep his voice steady. "Until I find it for you, I'm to be in your debt and follow you about Scotland like a hostage to your clan?"

Padruig pursed his lips as he thought this through, then gave Stuart a slight nod.

"And if I refuse?" Stuart hadn't battled for months against King Geordie's armies, Butcher Cumberland, and the Black Watch, nor survived weeks imprisoned and tortured, to succumb to the whims of Gair and Padruig. "Ye don't want to cross me, man," he said to Padruig.

Padruig's one good eye went icy and the hand that rested on the table tensed. Stuart kept his focus on that hand, which he knew could draw a knife in a flash.

Gair laughed, the sound lost in the general noise of the tavern. "I don't know why he's so set on retrieving this knife, lad, but Padruig don't set on a thing often. Best indulge him."

Stuart *could* fight them both—he'd taken on larger and tougher men. But together, Gair and Padruig made a formidable team, especially because they fought dirty, knew more tricks than a pair of weasels, and would not give up until they defeated their foe. They'd not survived this long without that sort of doggedness.

Stuart opened his hands in a gesture of surrender, pretending to relax, though the thought of facing Broc Macdonald and so many memories chilled him. "So be it."

Padruig's fist softened and the frost left his eye. He took a silent sip of ale.

"I warn you though, 'twon't be easy." Stuart directed his statement to Gair. "Fiona will want to keep a sharp eye on you."

"Aye." Gair deflated, his laughter dying, he probably imagining Fiona's eagle gaze fixed on his every move. "I thought as much."

~

Fiona's stomach growled as the savory odor of food being carried into the chamber wafted to her. She had her back to the door, only glimpsing the servant trundling in as she tidied her bag of belongings. She pushed the men's shirts and breeches she'd arranged to be left here with Carrie beneath her own clothes, so that anyone having a peek into the bag would see only her spare petticoats and stockings.

Una poked at the fire, not trusting the inn's staff to build it to her liking. The small room was gloriously warm, defying the snow swirling outside the dark window.

"Thank you," Fiona said to the servant. "Leave it on the table, and we'll have at it."

"Aye, miss," came the gravelly reply.

Fiona swung around. The servant, hunched in a homespun wool coat, glanced up at her, a twinkle in his blue eyes.

"Una," she said. "Will you wait outside a moment? Ask Carrie to give you something to eat."

Una took one look at Stuart Cameron bending over the food tray, folded her arms, and plunked herself onto a stool by the fire. "Nay," she said. "I'm staying."

CHAPTER 3

Fiona weighed the perils of Una remaining—she'd have to argue long and hard to send her maid away for a private moment with Stuart. Stuart clanked the plates on the tray, also making no move to leave.

Fiona, resigned, stepped past Stuart and closed the door.

"Your reputation, ma'am," Una said, aghast.

"Is beyond saving by this time," Fiona returned briskly. "Either everyone pities me as the sister of Broc Macdonald or they believe me a hussy, and nothing will change their opinion. It scarcely matters these days, does it?"

Stuart lifted his head. "When did you grow so cynical, love?"

His soft lilt threatened to shatter Fiona's heart. "When Highlanders died and my world was destroyed."

Stuart rose to his full height, his feigned obsequiousness falling away. "Why are you truly here, Fiona? Traveling alone?"

"Nothing I can tell you now." Fiona shivered as she indicated the walls and one small window. Anyone could listen, anyone could be in the pay of the Hanoverians, or hate the Jacobites for their own reasons. So many scores were being settled in the Uprising's aftermath.

Stuart nodded his understanding. "Will ye be returning home then?"

Fiona went to her bag and buckled it closed. "I don't know." Go back to Broc for Christmas and pretend to dote on him? She'd been gone for months this time, her travels ostensibly to visit friends all over the Highlands, which was partly true—she simply didn't mention what she and her friends got up to. Broc thought her a frivolous gadabout and had upbraided her the few times she'd returned. She hadn't been home now since June.

Stuart pushed his hair from his face in the endearing way she remembered. He was so tall, his broad shoulders in keeping with his size. He was a crazed fighter—she'd seen him do battle—and yet, the blunt hands that wielded a claymore and pistol so deftly could be gentle ...

Stuart's fingers left a sooty streak on his cheek. "When ye do go, I have a boon to ask." He darted a glance at Una, who fixed him with a scowl. "Take me with ye."

Fiona came out of her daze. "To Castle Mòr? Are ye mad? If Broc sees ye again, he'll kill you. He said so." She put her fists on her hips, her slim panniers swaying. "I recall *you* saying the same about him."

"Aye, but Padruig wants to go there. He thinks your

brother might have this dagger he's searching for. The pair of them sent me in here to persuade you."

"Oh." Fiona tamped down her sudden disappointment. She had no reason to believe Stuart would want to rekindle what they might have had if Prince Teàrlach hadn't arrived in the west. They'd only begun a few tendrils of passion, and then hell had come to them.

"If I find this bloody knife, I can go about my business," Stuart said. "Debt paid."

"Ye trust them?" Una asked in amazement. She'd never learned that retainers weren't to interrupt their employers—Una was a distant cousin, in any case, a member of Fiona's clan.

"Not really," Stuart answered. "But I'm ready to be shot of them. Gair isn't helping me out of the kindness of his heart."

"Aye, well, it might end in shooting," Una said darkly.

Gair and Padruig were no strangers to casual violence, Fiona knew. She also knew they would never betray a Jacobite Highlander. They might bleed that Highlander of all he had and steal anything left, but they were loyal Scots to the bone.

"I've come to beg ye." Stuart made a show of going down on his knees, which only made him slightly less tall.

Fiona's breath caught. She could go to him, place her hands on his shoulders, lean down and kiss him …

She sucked in air and nearly choked. "Aren't the Butcher's men looking for you?" Her words were cracked and dry. "It's dangerous for you to be in Scotland. Their men hunt everywhere."

"Aye, but I've come this far. 'Tisn't many more miles to your brother's home. And I'll continue playing the servant, a beast of burden."

Stuart was so far from being a beast of burden that Fiona wanted to laugh. "You might hide from Cumberland, but not from my brother," she pointed out.

"No matter. I'll discover if he has the dagger, give it to Padruig—or let Padruig convince your brother to let it go—and be off."

"Going where?" Fiona could barely voice the question.

Stuart shrugged. He climbed to his feet, towering over her once more.

How had Fiona come to be so close to him? She didn't remember moving, but now she stood only a yard away.

"Home for now." Stuart's words filled with emotion. "Back to my own lands."

"Where you'll be caught and captured."

Another shrug. "I'll do everything I can to prevent that, but I need to see to my house and people before I leave again. If I do. I'm tired of running, Fiona." His weariness touched her.

She closed her hands so they wouldn't tremble. If Stuart continued to stand so near and say her name like that, she'd be lost.

"I can't take ye to Broc. He'll kill ye."

Stuart rubbed his forehead, leaving another black streak. "Well, I'm going with or without ye, love. Be easier with ye."

Her irritation rose. "Bloody stubborn Scot."

"Aye, that's me." Stuart was inches from her, his big

hands clasping hers and lifting them to his lips. "Come with me, Fiona. Ye were so angry when I left ye, that ye might enjoy watching your brother trying to best me."

Never. Fiona had worried herself sick about Stuart from the moment he'd ridden away from the castle, laughing, rushing off to war.

Fiona pried her hands from his, hoping he couldn't see how much she was melting. "Never mind. I'll come with you. My intervention might keep ye alive." She tried to glower.

Stuart shot her a grin that was like sunshine breaking through clouds. "Even if it doesn't, I'll enjoy arguing with ye on the way." He made an exaggerated, courtly bow. "Ladies. Good evening. We leave on the morrow."

He turned up his collar, hunched himself down, opened the door, and tramped from the room, becoming one more servant in an inn full of travelers. The door closed, shutting out the noise.

"Ye aren't truly going to go to Castle Mòr with him, are ye?" Una asked in alarm.

Fiona checked her bag once more, making certain it was securely fastened. "Aye, that I am. What we have to do is on the way, anyway. Stuart or my brother might die if I don't go with him, and if I have a chance to prevent such a thing, I will."

"Humph," Una muttered, but thankfully said no more.

∾

The next morning, Christmas Eve, was bitterly cold but clear. Stuart, with Gair and Padruig, waited in the yard until Fiona and Una emerged. Una was bundled to her ears in misshapen wraps, Fiona in a loose dark skirt, long coat, and scarf.

Gair was ready to set off, clutching a long staff to trudge out of the yard, but Fiona forestalled him. "I must wait for my mount."

"Ye brought a horse?" Gair asked in amazement.

"I'm certainly not trudging through the snow on foot, sir." Fiona's green eyes widened over her scarf, and Stuart smothered a laugh.

One of the lads from the inn brought out a horse from the livery, a shaggy and sturdy mare. The lad moved to boost Fiona into the saddle, but Stuart reached her first. She gave him a startled look as he cupped his hand for her to step into, but she let him grasp her leg and lift her lightly to the mare's back. Fiona swung her leg over the saddle, revealing leather breeches beneath her skirt, riding astride like the resilient Scotswoman she was.

The contact with her shapely thigh and calf, even through the layers of clothing, warmed Stuart's blood. This was a woman made for loving, for lazing in bed with on a cold winter's day.

He'd take steps to ensure that happened once he was finished with Gair and Padruig. The war was over, Scotland in ruins. Fiona should not stay here. After he discovered whether his house was in one piece and retrieved some items from it, he'd take her to France, and they'd wait for time to pass. Together. His heart wrenched at the thought of leaving Scotland again, but he thought he could weather exile with Fiona.

Stuart gave Fiona's leg a pat. She glanced at him then

quickly away. Stuart couldn't see her cheeks beneath her scarf, but her forehead went a pretty pink.

Before Stuart could turn from her, Una more or less used him as a climbing tree to hoist herself behind Fiona, riding pillion. Stuart grunted as Una kicked him—surely she hadn't meant to do that—as she settled herself behind the saddle.

Stuart made certain both women were steady before Fiona took up the reins. She spoke softly to her mount, who flicked her ears at Fiona's voice. The beast had a wooly brown winter coat and a lighter brown mane and tail. A horse, not a pony, as rugged as the hills around them.

The stable boy tried to hand Fiona's bag to Una, but Stuart intercepted it and slung it over his shoulder. Fiona pretended nonchalance, but Una's silent concern was palpable. Interesting. What was in the bag they feared he'd see?

Stuart settled it on his back with his own small sack of belongings, and at last, they set off.

The bulk of the Macdonald realms lay on Scotland's western coast and the islands, which was why those clans had been among the first to support Prince Teàrlach—the prince had arrived on the islands and worked his way eastward, recruiting his army along the way.

Not all Macdonalds had joined the cause, which had created a bitter split in the clan, dividing families and friends. Fiona's brother had firmly stood against supporting the prince, and had finally taken up arms against his fellow Highlanders.

Broc Macdonald's castle lay south and west of Inverness, some twenty miles distant. Very near the lands of the Camerons. They were neighbors, if uneasy ones.

They couldn't skirt the long lake south of Inverness, because they'd run too close to Fort Augustus and other strongholds of the Hanoverians, who were still hunting Highlanders. Stuart doubted they'd give up even for Christmas.

No matter. Stuart knew these glens well, probably better than Gair and Padruig, who preferred hugging the coast so they could slip off over water. Stuart also knew the people in each village, though whether they'd hide him if asked, Stuart couldn't say. Too much fear lay in these lands, and no one wanted to be caught with one of the rebel Scots.

Fiona rode serenely along, gazing at the surprisingly clear sky, the hills rising to their right. Stuart walked next to Fiona's horse, where he could grab its bridle if the mare tried to bolt, though the horse seemed tame enough.

Gair, who walked a few paces ahead, following Stuart's directions, took them up a path that rose through woods, avoiding the more habitable places along the lake. Padruig brought up the rear. Unlike Gair, he used no walking staff and had strapped his small pack to his back, leaving his hands free.

Roads in the Highlands, once off the main thoroughfares, were more like wandering tracks made by cows sometime in the Middle Ages. Stuart's boots were coated in snow, ice, and mud before they'd gone a few miles.

"I see why ye're up there," he grumbled at Fiona. She hadn't said much except for bland remarks on how lucky they were in the weather. As this time of year was usually full of pissing rain or blinding snow, Stuart couldn't argue.

"It is drier on horseback, I grant," Fiona said. "And Piseag is so warm." She sank her gloved fingers into the horse's fur.

Stuart rumbled a laugh at the name. "Ye call her 'Kitten'?"

"What's wrong with that? She's gentle and soft."

"When I was a lad, a kitten climbed me and scratched my face all over."

Fiona's eyes crinkled as she studied him. "Poor Stuart. I don't see any scars on you. Well, it toughened ye for the army."

"Aye, Geordie's men were no match for that cat. She'd have had them begging for mercy."

"How did ye manage to have yourself captured, then?" Fiona asked, as though inquiring about why he'd been late for tea one afternoon. "If ye were so hardened by your cat?"

"Oh, you know. Helping a friend." The aftermath of Culloden rose in Stuart's mind. Jacobite soldiers were fleeing, after those who'd surrendered and laid down arms were slaughtered where they stood. His childhood friend, Calum, had been half dead, unable to run. Stuart had lingered to drag him away when four of Cumberland's men had surrounded them. Calum, already dying, had flung himself at the soldiers, and they'd cut him down. Stuart had attacked, bellowing a fierce cry, and had fought, enraged, before he'd been felled by a blow to the head.

"Still don't know why the soldiers didn't kill me outright," Stuart said, lightening his tone to hide his anger. "But they tied me up and took me off, first to an outbuilding, later marching me to a ship to journey south. Ended up in prison with Willie Mackenzie. Good thing. His brother Alec and the lady he married wrested us free, and I fled with all of them to Paris."

"Mackenzies?" Fiona asked in surprise. "I thought Will and Alec perished, along with the rest of the family."

"So did I, but there was Alec, opening the door of my cell, and Will chivvying us all out. Indestructible, is Will Mackenzie."

"It appears you are too." Fiona's voice lowered, "I read your name on the rolls. Captured. I was sure you'd be hanged."

"As was I, lady. But here I am."

She frowned at him, though she blinked, her eyes moist. "Walking right back into danger."

"I intend to stay out of it. Find Padruig his trophy and be about my business."

"Ah."

Stuart glanced quickly at Fiona, hoping he heard regret in her voice. He did not tell her that when he next vanished, he'd ask her to come with him. If she said no, he'd simply have to convince her, and he could come up with some very creative methods …

"Another reason for riding a horse," Fiona interrupted his thoughts. "Is that I can see farther than I can on foot. For instance, a few Black Watch and one English soldier are waiting for us around the next bend."

CHAPTER 4

Fiona's heart pumped faster as Stuart put his hand on Piseag's bridle to halt her, and whistled softly between his teeth. Gair hurried back to them, and Padruig gathered close.

Fiona tried to stay calm, forcing herself not to beg Stuart to hide, to flee back to the inn. He could blend in with the throng there and escape during the Christmas revelry.

Stuart's face set in stubborn lines, his blue eyes quiet as he withdrew into himself. Fiona watched him leave the carefree, laughing, impetuous Highlander behind and become the honed and deadly soldier.

They stood in a thick stand of trees, the land sloping sharply upward on their right, downward on the left. At the scrape of boots of the approaching soldiers, Stuart left the track, fading noiselessly into the uphill woods, his dark coat blending with the black rocks and boles of trees among the snow.

Padruig seized Piseag's bridle, and Una moved restlessly behind Fiona.

The soldiers rounded the bend and stopped in surprise. No officers, Fiona thought with relief. Just infantrymen, possibly heading for their camp or perhaps even Balthazar's inn, anticipating a warm room and a draught of ale.

No worries that the soldiers would search her bag, Fiona reflected. Stuart still had it on his back and he was gone.

The three Black Watch, in their kilts—the tartan ban did not extend to them—looked more annoyed than worried when they beheld Fiona and party. Fiona's idea that they were heading to camp or the inn to go off-duty solidified.

The Englishman with them, in the red coat of Something-or-Other Foot, appeared as anxious to push past them as the others, but it was his duty to stop and question any Scots person on the road.

The four formed a barrier across the track, the Englishman slightly to one side, as though ready to let the Black Watch deal with any trouble.

One of the Black Watch soldiers lifted his rifle from his shoulder and aimed it vaguely at them. "No farther. Who are ye, and what's your business on this road?"

"I don't call it much of a road." Gair spat to the side of it. "We're taking this lady safely to shelter. It's brutal cold, if ye'd not noticed."

The man had the sharp blue eyes and fair hair of a Highlander, his accent putting him from the north and east. "What lady, and what shelter?"

"This lady." Gair jerked his thumb at Fiona. "Whatever shelter we can find. Any houses the way you've come?"

"Only burned ones." The man smiled a little over the barrel of his rifle.

Fiona lost her temper. These were Scotsmen who'd turned on their own people, burning homes of those suspected of hiding Jacobites, throwing entire families out with nowhere to go.

She dragged her scarf from her mouth, letting the cold burn her lips. "I see you there, Iver MacGregor," she said to another of the Black Watch who hovered behind the man with the rifle. He was thinner than the others, with brown hair under his bonnet, and scraggly whiskers on his face to match. "What would your mother say about that beard? Ye should grow it out or cut it off entirely."

Padruig remained stoic, but Gair shot Fiona an alarmed look, trying to silence her. The Englishman and the soldier who hadn't spoken struggled to hide grins.

"Fiona?" Iver bleated. "I mean … Miss Macdonald? What are you doing out here in the weather?"

"Trying to get *out* of the weather. But you and your friends are blocking my way."

Iver's mouth popped open, which was its usual position. Iver MacGregor lived in the next glen from Fiona's family home, and he and Broc had played together as children. Iver looked perpetually bewildered, had even when he'd come out of his shell enough to dance with Fiona one Hogmanay, before he'd joined the Black Watch.

"We can't let none pass," Iver explained as though Fiona hadn't heard about the Uprising. "Rebels about."

The Black Watch leader lowered his rifle but didn't move, seeming happy to let Iver speak for all of them.

Fiona made a show of looking around. "I see no Highlanders here. Only these men I hired to see me through. You know them. Gair Murray and Padruig."

Iver flushed, and the others shuffled, uncomfortable. Most people in the Highlands had bought smuggled goods from Gair and Padruig. The minute Gair was arrested, he could reveal what he'd sold not only to every soldier whose duty it was to stamp out smuggling, but to their superiors as well, all the way up the chain of command.

Iver stepped closer to the horse, on the side opposite Padruig, and peered up at Fiona. "Ye trust them?"

"I do to lead me true until they receive their pay at the end of the road. I'm only going home. My brother is ill, as you might have heard."

Iver nodded, brow furrowing. "Aye, he took injury at Falkirk, I recall. Give him me best."

"I will. Now, shall you let me pass?"

The Black Watch leader roused to life. "Sorry, ma'am. Orders. Everyone on the road is to be searched."

"Very well." Fiona nodded to Una, who started to slide down. Padruig caught Una and set her on her feet, but Fiona swung off herself, not waiting for assistance. "Be quick about it. I'd like to be indoors before nightfall."

Thank heavens for Stuart. She could be serene, knowing the soldiers wouldn't find the extra clothes and food she carried, would never realize what she intended to do with them.

Gair was less sanguine. "Ye can see I'm not carrying

guns or a casket of gold, can't ye? Will ye rob me of the few coins I have? I'm reduced to escorting a woman across the Highlands for pay. Take pity on me."

Iver winced. "Sorry, Gair. I'll make it quick."

Iver found four knives, two flasks of whisky, and a few English gold sovereigns in Gair's pockets, but nothing that seemed to alarm anyone. Padruig had one knife and a flask and that was all.

With Iver's persuasion, they allowed Una and Fiona to turn out their own pockets, showing they carried only dried meat, bread, and cheese for the journey.

The leader clicked Gair's two gold coins together. "We might have to confiscate this. Could be the spoils of smuggling."

"Now, hang on—" Gair blustered.

"Give them to him, Gair." Fiona kept up her air of an inconvenienced highborn lady as she turned back to her horse. "I'll give you the cost at journey's end."

She allowed Padruig to give her a leg-up into the saddle, settling herself and paying no more attention to the men, as Una was lifted on behind her.

The leader grinned, and the coins disappeared. Gair snarled. Padruig stepped to Gair and simply looked at him. Gair subsided.

"Give my best to your mum, Iver," Fiona said graciously. "Good day, gentlemen."

Padruig grasped the bridle again, though Fiona held the reins, and led the mare past the soldiers. The Englishman and the two other Black Watch seemed pleased with their chance encounter. Iver saluted Fiona wistfully.

"Take care, Fiona. Perhaps I'll see ye at your brother's at Hogmanay?"

"Perhaps." Fiona nodded down at him, as though it made no difference to her.

She managed to remain composed as Padruig led her on, Gair following, but her mouth was dry, her limbs trembling. She adjusted her scarf over her nose, its warmth welcoming.

Would the soldiers see Stuart? Hear him? Shoot him outright? And where had Stuart gone? He knew these woods and valleys better than most. Would he vanish over the mountains, never to be seen again?

Her heart pounded, and her fingers twitched. She wanted to urge Piseag to run, run, run, so she could find Stuart but knew that would be the height of foolishness.

They rounded the bend. The soldiers did not follow, though Fiona did not risk glancing back to see whether they watched.

Padruig and Gair kept up a steady but not rapid pace, Gair raising his voice in a badly out of tune song. Another mile went by, and another. They saw no more soldiers, and Fiona began to relax.

Fiona also did not see Stuart. They traveled for an hour, the road leaving the hills and striking over a glen toward mountains beyond and the castle where Broc Macdonald had retreated, nursing his injury.

Clouds began to blot the sky. Fiona would have to turn aside soon, as she'd promised, though how she'd fulfill her mission without the bag Stuart had taken she did not know. She could only do her best.

They stopped in the shelter of a tree to water the horse

in the nearby stream, Padruig breaking ice with his boot. In a low voice, Fiona explained to the two men what she meant to do. As predicted, Gair argued, but Padruig gruffly agreed and stared Gair to silence. Then they went on.

Fiona saw no sign of Stuart as the clouds gathered, and she realized as the miles went by, that he was truly gone.

∼

Stuart, who'd been shadowing Fiona and party, pulled his coat close against the growing wind. He knew they were heading for Broc's castle in the next glen, so he could simply hurry there and wait for them. But leaving Fiona to the mercy of Gair and Padruig, not to mention any Hanoverian soldiers lurking about, did not appeal to him.

Stuart was surprised, then, when Fiona turned off the small road that would take her to her brother's castle, and wended her way up a path toward a tiny crack between two tall mountains.

CHAPTER 5

Stuart followed at a discreet distance as Fiona's horse went higher into the foothills, around a stand of snow-covered boulders, and out of sight.

There was nothing back there. Stuart knew every nook and cranny of this part of the Highlands, especially so close to his own lands. No one lived in that bleak area of the mountains, and no road led through the rocks. It was a dead end.

The phrase made him shudder. Stuart scanned the open ground between himself and the boulders, then sped his steps to cross the snowy valley, not slowing until he'd reached the rocks behind which Fiona had ridden.

The bag he carried weighed on his back. He'd had a look inside and found Fiona's things, but also men's clothing, secondhand and worn, the kind laborers would wear. Several sets of them. He'd studied them in puzzlement—why on earth was she riding around the Highlands with such gear?

Stuart reached the outcropping in time to see Fiona,

the horse, Una, Padruig, and Gair, vanish in a cleft in the rocks. Stuart skirted the snowy boulders and approached.

When he started into the black shadow between the rocks, he suddenly found himself staring down the tip of Padruig's knife. Stuart halted, the point against his nose.

Padruig recognized Stuart, blinked, and relaxed. "Ye'd better come in."

A blanket had been tacked between tall rocks, forming a door of sorts against the cold. Behind it, Stuart found Highlanders, half a dozen of them.

The men had grubby, bearded faces and weariness in their eyes. Stuart recognized a few of them, the rest he did not. Retainers and men, foot soldiers of Prince Teàrlach's army. Those who'd fought and then fled for their lives when the word came down that no quarter was to be given.

Fiona glanced at Stuart. "Good. You've come."

She might have been welcoming him to a small garden party she'd arranged. Saying nothing more, she reached for the bag Stuart slid from his shoulder.

Fiona plunked the bag down and opened it, digging past a flash of women's underclothes to pull out breeches, shirts, and coats. Una busily helped.

"I should have things to fit everybody," she said as she laid out the garments. "The coats might be a bit small, but they're the best that could be found."

"Aye, well, I'll have me tailor sew me a new one." One Highlander flashed his teeth in a grin. "Next time I visit him in London."

A few guffaws sounded, but mostly these men were exhausted.

"Gair," Stuart said quietly. "Hand round your flask."

Gair turned innocent eyes to him. "What flask is that?"

"Do it, lad," Padruig growled.

Gair immediately pulled a battered tin bottle from his pocket. He opened it, releasing the pungent odor of whisky.

"*Uisge beatha*," one man said in reverence. "Thought I'd never taste fine malt again."

"And ye won't now, I wager," Stuart said.

The man took the flask, drank, and coughed. "You're right, there. Tastes like me gran's washing-up water."

The others laughed but they reached eagerly for the flask in turn. Fiona handed them the food she'd purchased at the tavern for the journey, all of her share. Stuart moved to stop her, but Fiona's face was set, and he knew he'd only begin an argument.

The mystery of why she carried the clothing was solved. Now to the mystery of how she'd known these men would be here.

"We encountered Black Watch about seven miles to the northeast," Fiona told them as they ate. "They were heading toward Inverness. Tonight will be a good time to slip out and make your way to Kinloch Hourn. A ship will be there to take ye to Skye."

"Straight through your brother's lands," one man pointed out. "Skirting them, anyway."

Fiona nodded. "I will keep Broc occupied, and he'll never notice. I'll burn down the castle if I have to."

More laughter. "I believe ye," the man continued. "Why don't you come with us, lass? We could use a soft face to light our way."

Amid nods from the other men, Fiona jerked her thumb at Stuart. "I have to help this one out of trouble first. Will take all my skill, I think."

"Aye, Stuart Cameron is nothing but trouble," the man said. "Where've ye been, lad? Haven't seen ye since Culloden. Thought you were dead."

"I was helping His Majesty discover how many knives can cut into a Highlander before he betrays his fellows."

Fiona glanced at him, her eyes glittering in the darkness.

"And what is the answer?" the Highlander asked.

Stuart shrugged. "Don't know. I never let them get to the end. I decided to quit playing and legged it."

The chuckles came again. Most of the men were happily eating the meager meal, shared exactly between them.

Padruig, who'd been standing guard at the door, ducked inside. "We should not linger."

"True." Fiona re-latched her bag. "Any messages for your families, lads?"

They all had something to say, though more than one begged Fiona not to endanger their loved ones by revealing where the men would go.

"Never worry," Fiona said cheerfully. "I am quite discreet."

"We thank ye, lady," the lead Highlander said. "We hate to take your charity, but sometimes a man grows desperate."

"Not charity," Stuart broke in. "It's Christmas."

"Aye, and that makes us the three wise men," Gair said. "We come bearing gifts, as I like to say."

"But you're about to go see King Herod," the leader returned. "Broc Macdonald, who once pretended to be a friend."

"A friend to all of us," Stuart said. "I think, when he discovered I had designs on his sister, he went a bit mad." Fiona flushed but did not correct him.

"He was mad before that," the Highlander said. "I've known him all me life. Don't wish him well from me. My apologies, lass."

Fiona shook her head. "The times have changed us all. My brother is an arse. I *will* tell him that."

Laughter rang out, softened at the last minute. "God bless ye," another man said. "Happy Christmas."

"Happy Christmas." Fiona bathed them all in a warm smile and slid out of the shelter, Stuart holding the blanket for her.

The leader caught hold of Stuart before he could go. "Take care of that one," he murmured, his breath sharp with Gair's whisky. "She's an angel of mercy. But if she's caught helping men like us …"

"I won't let her be," Stuart said with conviction.

He waited until Gair retrieved his empty flask, then followed him out.

Padruig was about to assist Fiona onto her horse, but Stuart waved him off. Padruig ducked aside, taking the bag from Una under her very watchful eye.

Stuart turned Fiona to him, the two of them resting against Piseag's warm flank. Before she could speak, he tilted her face to his and kissed her.

∽

THE KISS TOOK FIONA'S BREATH AWAY. SHE'D MISSED Stuart with every beat of her heart in the long year since she'd seen him last, and his presence now both elated and weakened her. His arms hard on her back kept her upright as his tongue tangled hers, he tasting of whisky and the bracing cold.

But his mouth held heat, his breath scalding her cheek. Fiona dug her fingers into his coat, the rough wool laced with his warmth. Her body ran with fire, need squeezing her, as well as joy that he was here, unhurt, and alive.

She felt the gazes of Padruig, Gair, and Una on them, none of the three ready to politely turn away. Stuart didn't seem to care. He scooped Fiona up into him, kissing his fill. Piseag remained solidly at her side, as though the mare understood Fiona needed her to prop her up.

A sharp blast of wind made Stuart lift his lips from Fiona's. He gazed down at her, his blue eyes like pieces of aquamarine. He was Scotland, its sky and bluster, its strength and wildness.

He slowly released her, his breath coming fast. "Are ye well, lass?"

Fiona didn't know. She never would be, not until Stuart was completely safe.

"Yes," she whispered.

Stuart traced her cheek. His leather glove was coarse against her skin, but his touch was gentle as could be.

He abruptly stooped down, grasping Fiona's booted foot to boost her up into the saddle. He lifted Una behind her, while Una gazed over her scarf with all the scorn of a Viking queen.

Stuart caught Piseag's reins and turned the horse. "Come on," he said to Gair and Padruig. "We should get ourselves indoors before nightfall."

~

THE FIRST WISPS OF SNOW BEGAN TO FALL AS THEY crossed the last open valley and into the fold of mountain where lay the Macdonald family home.

Fiona eyed the glen with mixed feelings. She'd played here in her happy girlhood, knew sorrow with the deaths of first her mother then her father, and grew frustrated when she realized her brother saw her as a commodity to be married off. A clanswoman could be used to strengthen ties with other clans. Broc hadn't intended for her to fall for a Cameron, especially one with Jacobite sympathies—Broc believed that being loyal to King Geordie would help him rise in profit and status.

Stuart had said very little to her since his impetuous kiss, resuming the trek through the cold wind. Fiona hadn't quite recovered, and wasn't certain she would. The kiss had staggered her, opening up places she'd forced closed.

Her thoughts went back to the last kiss she'd shared with Stuart, September of the previous year, before Teàrlach reached Edinburgh and took it over. They'd had a grand ball at Castle Mòr, Broc's way of saying he wasn't afraid. He'd invited both Jacobites and loyalists, as though daring anyone to make trouble. The Camerons had come, Stuart in their lead, and with him had been Mal, Alec, and Will Mackenzie.

Fiona had laughed and danced with them all,

knowing in her heart disaster was near. Those supporting Teàrlach were too confident, those opposing too scornful. Their arrogance would clash violently, and she'd been right.

Stuart had swung her out of the Scots dance and into a hall outside the ballroom. He'd leaned her against a wall, his fiery hair loosening from its queue, his body warm in the night.

"Come with me, lass," he'd whispered. "When all this is over and Scotland ruled by its own king, come home with me. We'll have a grand celebration, with you as my lady."

It wasn't exactly a proposal of marriage but Fiona had known that was what he meant.

They'd kissed, long and passionately, Stuart's hands on her waist, one coming up to cup her breast. The taste of him had lingered from that day to this, brought to life once more by their kiss outside the shelter.

Fiona hadn't given him an answer that night. The future had been so uncertain, and she hadn't wanted to upset Broc.

Stuart had come to her one more time before he'd left to join Teàrlach's army, and Broc had threatened to kill him.

Ye think I'll let me sister run off with a bloody Jacobite? What will ye drag her to, a hovel while you hide as a traitor?

'Twill be a damned better fate for her than being forced to marry one of your toadies, Stuart had growled. *Have the grace to follow Teàrlach and die like a man for your lands. Let Fiona be laird—she'll be far better at it than you.*

Broc had let out a snarl of fury and drawn his dagger. Fiona, in alarm, had stepped between the two men.

I'm going nowhere, she'd shouted. *With either of you!*

She hadn't dared storm from the room, or Broc might have gone at Stuart. Stuart would have defended himself, and blood would have been spilled.

Stuart had rounded on Fiona, his red and green plaid swinging. *Come with me, lass, away from this rotten bastard who'll drag ye into the muck with him.*

He'll drag ye to a Jacobite dunghill, Broc had countered. *Go with him and be damned to ye. You'll both be hanged soon enough.*

Behind his bluster, Fiona had seen Broc's fear, his pain from the death of their parents that time had not erased. Broc worried for Fiona, sure that Teàrlach would lose, and she being with Stuart would doom her. He didn't want to lose Fiona as well.

Stuart had glared at Fiona, his fury at Broc plain. Behind it, he also had fear—that he'd never see Fiona again.

I can't, Stuart. Fiona had let her voice go soft. *When it's over, and if you're alive, you come back to me.*

It will be over swiftly, Stuart had promised. *In weeks, lass.*

In weeks, you'll be dead, Broc had declared, his head up, his arrogance high.

Stuart had laughed. *Then I'll never have to see you again.*

If I do see ye, I'll kill ye. Broc had pointed his dagger at Stuart, determination in his eyes.

Stuart had laughed again, spun on his heel, and was gone, the sound of his boots ringing on the stones.

Fiona hadn't worried much, not then. Stuart had been correct—Teàrlach had already been poised to take Edinburgh, and then he'd quickly won at Prestonpans. Stuart would come marching back soon, and Fiona would leave her home to be with him. She imagined that once the Jacobites had the upper hand and Teàrlach's father was installed as king, Broc would switch sides with blinding rapidity.

But none of that had happened. France's promised support had vanished in the fickle wind. Teàrlach's army had eventually been crushed, so many men dying, and for what? For a callow young prince who'd proved he had no idea what he was doing against a force that far outnumbered his.

Now proud Highland men hid in makeshift hideaways, dependent on the charity of Fiona and women like her.

Stuart hadn't returned to her. She'd read of his capture, knew he'd soon die, and tried to bury the anguish in her heart.

Until she'd glanced up at the inn yesterday afternoon, and beheld him.

This time, she knew, she could never let him go.

∽

STUART EXPECTED, AS THEY APPROACHED THE CASTLE, that the giant door would open, and a dozen soldiers, egged on by Broc, would pour out and surround them. They'd not even bother arresting Stuart—they'd stab him through immediately, or wait a bit while they built a gallows to hang him. But nothing like that happened.

The castle, as good castles that had survived from the 1400s were wont, squatted on a hill overlooking two valleys. A long road wound to it, the approach visible from the tall windows.

The castle itself was a square tower that rose five floors, with a two-story addition built in the 1600s in front of that. The newer wing held the great hall, where Stuart had danced with Fiona in happier times.

Gray-brown stone made the castle appear to be yet another rock thrusting up through the snow. Stuart saw no light in any window, no sign of habitation.

Perhaps Broc had given up cold drafts and moved to a more solid house in Edinburgh—Stuart couldn't help hoping. Fiona would take over the castle and liven it up. Stuart always said she'd be better at running the place than Broc.

He glanced at her, but she'd pulled her scarf over her face again, a hood covering her hair. He couldn't see her in the darkness, couldn't tell what she thought of bringing Stuart to her home.

Would Broc kill Stuart right away? Or philosophically reflect on how much life had changed both men?

Stuart stifled a laugh. Broc wasn't the reflecting sort.

No one challenged them as they slogged on. The castle loomed high, and Stuart's breath quickened as they climbed the steep hill toward it. Were they walking into an ambush? Or would they find an empty and deserted castle?

A gate in the center of the outer wall led, Stuart remembered, to a courtyard and the great hall. The gate was closed, likely bolted for the night.

Fiona nudged Piseag, turning her flank to the gate, which Fiona pounded with her fist.

Stuart squashed his hat down on his head, pulling up the collar of his coat. With any luck, he would still pass for Gair's lackey. He'd find Padruig's knife—or convince the man it wasn't here—and move on to his own house.

After a long wait, Gair moving restlessly, the gate creaked open, and a pale face peered out. "Who's there?" a hoarse voice asked.

"Marcas?" Fiona sounded astonished. "Why on earth are you answering the door? Where is everyone?"

"Miss Fiona." The name was exhaled in relief. A thin man with graying red hair pushed open the door, his lined face eerie by the flickering light of his lantern. "They've all run off, miss. Well, most have. Terrified they'll be taken as Jacobites. Or killed by Jacobites."

"Truly?" Fiona asked in indignation.

Stuart wasn't very surprised. Broc had never engendered loyalty, the man being so distrusting himself. Stuart wondered, with a qualm, if he'd find the same situation at his home.

"Aye. It's a sad state of affairs," Marcas said. "Not long after ye left the last time, they decided they'd had enough, and up and went. Come in—the laird will need to see you."

Not *will want to see you* or *be happy to see you*, but *need to*. *Hmm*.

"Then we'll go to him right away. *Tapadh leibh*, Marcas."

She'd merely said *thank you*, but Marcas peered up at her in worry. "Never speak Erse here, Miss. Ye know the laird doesn't like us to."

"Nonsense. Where is he?"

Una had already dismounted, and now Fiona swung her leg over the saddle. Stuart caught her and lifted her to the ground. Fiona glanced at him gratefully and stepped inside the gate, leaving Stuart to handle the horse, as a servant should.

The courtyard was deserted. Even this late, with snow starting, Stuart would expect to see it a hive of activity. Broc was a laird, which meant he was the main landholder in this area. He'd not only have tenants but all the workers who kept the castle running—gamekeeper, farm steward, blacksmith, cooks. Various other servants should be there to make certain the laird and his family had plenty of food and firewood this cold winter's night.

No one but Marcas, whom Stuart remembered was Broc's valet, appeared. Marcas ushered them across the silent courtyard. Stuart broke away to take Piseag to a stall inside the walls, quickly stripping off her saddle and bridle, and making sure she had food in her manger.

He caught up to Fiona and party as they entered the new addition of the castle and the empty great hall. His footsteps echoed as they crossed the slates where Fiona had danced with Stuart to the merry tunes of fiddles and the thump of drums.

"*Everyone* is gone?" Fiona asked.

"All but me and a few others." Marcas sounded tired. "I tell the laird he should go, to Edinburgh perhaps, or London, but he doesn't listen. His cousins say the same."

"Cousins?" Apprehension filled Fiona's voice.

"Aye. Neilan and Tavin Macdonald have been coming and going some months now. Just yesterday they arrived for Christmas"

"Oh, no." Fiona turned from Marcas and fled the great hall, hurrying into the dark passageway beyond.

CHAPTER 6

Fiona hastened through the short corridor that connected the new hall to the old castle, built so the laird would not get wet or too cold traveling from his private chambers to the public area.

She went up another flight of stairs in the old building to the inner hall, which was much smaller than the new one, about twenty feet long and ten wide. The ceiling had been renovated in the last century and now contained dark carved beams that lent some warmth to the gray stones.

Or would lend warmth, if there was any light or heat to the place. A smudge of rushlight glowed at one end of a table, haloing the faces of three men—Broc and next to him, the cousins, Tavin and Neilan, reprobates and parasites. They being here could not bode well.

"Broc?"

At the sound of Fiona's voice, the man at the head of the table jumped to his feet. He tottered, grabbed a stick next to him, and hobbled forward.

"Fiona?" Relief tinged his voice. "Is it you? I'd given up."

Fiona grew cautious, but Broc sounded genuinely glad to see her. He stumbled toward her, leaning heavily on the stick, and caught her in an embrace.

"It is a happy Christmas indeed," he breathed in her ear.

"Cousin Fiona." Tavin rose from the bench he'd been sitting on and made his way to her. His brother Neilan also rose but remained at the table. "Welcome. How fortunate."

"Fortunate?" Fiona's suspicions immediately rose. The last time she'd seen Tavin, he'd been trying to convince her that marrying him and giving him all her money was a grand idea.

"Aye. We're trying to persuade Broc to take ship for the Americas. Better for him than limping around here. He can start a new life in the colonies."

"Can he?" Fiona skewered Tavin with a gaze. Tavin was tall and admittedly good-looking, and he thought much of himself. He dressed in the English style—breeches and brocade frock coat that was far out of place in this ancient setting. He wore a wig, white and sleek over his true dark hair.

"And what happens to Castle Mòr if my brother leaves the country?" Fiona asked as though merely curious.

"Well." Tavin attempted affability. "We're the closest male heirs, you know. If you go with Broc, we'll take good care of it. If you stay …" Tavin took a step closer to her, and Broc had to move out of his way. "The castle is yours, of course. But you'll need a husband, won't you?"

One more step, until Fiona could smell the powder on his wig. She heard a rumble, and then Stuart was there, his hands full of Tavin's coat, hauling the man away from Fiona and to the nearest stone pillar.

Neilan, who was even more of a fop than his brother, his wig decorated with four green silk ribbons, squeaked, and Broc hastened back to Fiona. "See here, you. Unhand him. Fiona, who is this man? I can have him arrested."

Stuart raised Tavin halfway up the pillar and let him go. Tavin landed on his feet, but his high-heeled shoes turned under him, and he staggered, grabbing for the pillar to hold him up.

Stuart turned around, pulling off his battered hat and throwing it to the ground.

"*Feasgar Mhath*, Broc Macdonald. How have ye been keeping yourself?"

～

As had the creaky retainer, Broc cringed as Stuart bade him a good evening in the Scots language. Stuart thought Broc was more upset about hearing his mother tongue than seeing Stuart Cameron returned from the dead. The Macdonald cousins were equally dismayed by the words, but Stuart saw no recognition in their eyes.

"What are ..." Broc trailed off and swallowed. "Fiona?"

"'Tis not my doing." Fiona unwound her scarves, though it was scarcely warmer in here than outdoors. Her face appeared, flushed with cold. "I found him on the way home. Now—it has been a long journey and I am hungry. Is there food? Lights?"

"Everyone has gone," Broc said. He did not look well, his face pale in the flickering rushlight, and he clutched the stick as though it was all that kept him on his feet. He shot a fearful glance to Padruig and Gair, who'd followed Stuart in. "Deserted me. Only three are left—the gamekeeper, Donia in the kitchen, and Marcas."

Fiona's eyes went wide. "Good heavens. Only three people to have the caring of you? Can ye not shift yourself to the kitchen and carve a bit of bread and cheese? I assume Donia is doing the cooking. She was kitchen assistant when I left."

"Yes, she is carrying on." Broc's voice was a near whisper.

"Sit down, man," Stuart advised. "'Tis clear ye can barely stand. There's no shame in it. Ye took a hit in battle."

Broc sank to his high-backed wooden chair—the laird's chair. All else around the table were benches. Tavin, who'd finally recovered himself and brushed off his coat, smirked at Broc. Tavin hadn't fought in the war, had likely never picked up a musket in his life.

"What about our tenants?" Fiona asked. "Are they well? Sitting in warm, snug houses, or ones with holes in the roofs?"

"Don't know. Most have gone. Marcas says many have turned to the cities to find work and won't be coming back."

He was a broken man. Stuart again wondered if he'd

find his own home like this one. Deserted, empty, all having fled in fear.

"Which is why *we* should take it over," Tavin said. "Ye don't need farms, ye need sheep. Wool fetches a nice price, and sheep don't fuss over their roofs. Times are changing, Broc. King George beat the Scots idiots who want to live in the dark ages. *You* picked the right side. Go off to the colonies and leave it to us. You'll see."

"This is my home," Broc said weakly.

"And mine." Fiona fixed Tavin with her steely gaze. "Make yourself useful, you two. Go down to the kitchens and see what's to eat."

"Ha," Tavin said. "We're not lackeys."

"Very well. I'll go." Fiona tossed down her scarves and turned toward a door that led to the stairs.

Tavin started after her. Stuart gave him a cold stare, and Tavin quickly backed away. Stuart ducked into the stone stairwell Fiona had entered, holding the walls to steady himself as the stairs spiraled downward.

He'd left Padruig and Gair in the hall, but he did not fear for them. With any luck they'd terrify Tavin and his brother into disappearing into the night.

Stuart caught up with Fiona in a passage that connected storage rooms to the kitchen.

"Are ye all right, lass?" he asked in a low voice.

"They're leeches," she said furiously. "Sucking us dry."

"I see that. Family can be hell." Stuart cupped her shoulders. "It's been a long ride, and ye've done much." He brushed a finger over her smooth cheek. "Your compassion astonishes me."

Fiona shrugged, but he saw a flicker of darkness in

her eyes. "I can't not help Highlanders who are trying to survive. They fought so bravely, while my cousins sit on their cushions, eat sweetmeats, and tend to their wigs."

Stuart flashed her a grin. "Ye have hidden depths."

"They need to stay hidden, don't they? Or I'll be arrested and those lads hunted down."

"Aye, as you say. How many others have ye helped while I sat on my … cushion … in prison?"

"I don't know. Dozens."

"How do ye find them? If you'll let me ask? How did those lads come to hide in the rocks near Càrn Eige?"

"They were sent word." Fiona kept her voice quiet, still wary of being overheard. "And I received word that they were there. No one pays much attention to what women get up to. It's wives and sisters and mothers all over the Highlands who find the men and make sure they're fed, clothed, and provided a path to safety. Supplies are left by those who can obtain them at places like the inn where you found me. I and a few others coordinate it."

Stuart lightly caressed her shoulders. "They are correct—you are an angel of mercy."

Fiona's face softened, and she rested her hands on his chest. "If I'd known you were in prison, I'd have tried to find out where and have you released. I'm so sorry."

Stuart stared down at her in amazement. "If ye'd poked around, ye might have been arrested, or … King Geordie's soldiers got up to terrible things. I'm glad ye didn't know. But it's all right now."

"Is it?" Fiona's eyes sparkled with tears. "I've always thought of my home as a refuge, even with the arguments I have with Broc. Now it's too sad. Broc …"

"Aye, he's not well. He needs to be somewhere warm where he can heal."

She stiffened. "Not Antigua. I'm not letting Tavin send him off to the colonies."

"I meant warm and snug, not hot and malarial."

"Oh. Then what...?"

Stuart forestalled her words by tilting her face up and kissing her. He couldn't resist with her standing so close, she shrugging off her sacrifices to assist defeated men, never mind the grave danger to herself.

He got lost in the kiss, Fiona rising to him, her arms going around his neck. Fiona held on, her body flowing to his, her lips parting. Stuart kissed her leisurely, tasting her, letting the wanting he'd bottled up surge through him.

Fiona gave and gave of herself, assuming a brisk air to keep others from wounding her. So few gave to *her*.

But Stuart was here for her now. Coming to this castle and seeing Broc Macdonald had revealed to him exactly what he needed to do.

He eased away from the kiss, tracing her lower lip with a gentle thumb.

Fiona drew in a breath. Stuart expected her to berate him, but she only met his gaze with a steady one, opening herself to him.

He read Fiona's hurts and fears over the last year as she'd watched Scotsmen and Scotswomen become intoxicated and then destroyed by Prince Teàrlach's cause, saw her brother come home wounded, his spirits ebbing.

She'd also believed she'd lost Stuart—he saw the sharp devastation his disappearance had caused. He pulled Fiona close, burying his face in the curve of her neck.

"Never again," he whispered. "We'll never be parted again."

Fiona's relieved sigh made his heart sing. Her arms came around him, enclosing him, shielding him. Stuart had missed her with a mad intensity.

After a long time, he lifted away. "That is, unless ye want to see the back of me."

He kept his words light, but he waited in trepidation for Fiona to agree.

Fiona touched his face, running her fingertips over his unshaved whiskers. She laughed softly, dissolving his fears. "'Tis the front of you I like seeing." She sent him an arch look and took his hand. "Though the back of ye can look well too. Now, I am truly hungry. Shall we feast?"

∾

THEY DID NOT FIND MUCH IN THE LARDER, BUT EVEN the meager pickings of bannocks and drippings, slices of cold mutton, and a few wilted greens seemed a feast after the long day of travel.

Donia, the cook's assistant, had taken over and was not happy about it. "I want to go live with me mum," she said. "But I hate to leave the master. He's all in, the poor love."

Fiona had never heard her brother called a "poor love." Broc had always been arrogant and commanding, even after his injury, but tonight, she'd found him a pathetic wreck.

Una, who'd entered the kitchen after taking Fiona's things to her room, began assisting Donia without a word.

"We'll feed him up," Fiona promised. She took the tray that Donia had piled high with food and crockery, but Stuart immediately relieved her of it.

"You're good to stay, Donia," Stuart said. "I'm thinking the others will return when the countryside is calmer. The cities are full of smoke and hardship, no place to raise a family."

"I tried to tell them." Donia's eyes filled. "I hope you're right, sir."

"I am." Stuart strode from the kitchen with all the confidence Fiona remembered. If he said a thing would happen, it would.

Stuart led the way up the stairs, carrying the heavy tray as though it weighed nothing. When they reentered the hall, Gair was busy trying to interest the two cousins in purchasing a silver snuffbox in pristine condition. Fiona did not want to know where he'd obtained it. Possibly a perfectly legal transaction, but then, this was Gair.

Broc's eyes brightened when the tray landed on the table and Stuart began handing out dishes like a trained servant. Tavin and Neilan hadn't quite worked out yet who he was.

"Thank you, sister," Broc said. "I could use some grub."

"Not too much," Tavin said quickly. "You're weak. Broth is better for a man in your condition."

"Bollocks." Stuart plunked a good portion of the mutton and bannocks onto a plate and slid it in front of

Broc. "He needs feeding up. Have you been starving the man?"

Broc lifted his knife and started sawing at the mutton, using the tip to shovel the meat into his mouth. "Been a long time since I had a full meal."

Fiona turned her glare to her cousins, but spoke to Broc, "Well, you needn't worry any more about that. I've come to look after you."

"As you should." Broc's automatic reply made him sound like his old self, the high-handed laird certain Fiona should obey his every command. She'd never understood why he'd assume she'd listen.

Stuart dished out a plate for Fiona and himself and also for Gair and Padruig, who had no qualms about joining them at the table. Neilan continued to gaze covetously at the snuffbox. Neither cousin noticed Stuart wasn't serving them until Stuart sat down and began eating.

"Steady on, man," Tavin said. When Stuart ignored him, Tavin let out a growl and reached for the food—what was left of it. He took as much as he could for himself and shoved the mostly empty platters toward Neilan.

Stuart had found a carafe of whisky in the kitchen and now poured a dollop for everyone at the table except Tavin and Neilan.

They ate in silence for a time, during which Padruig shot a hard look at Stuart. Fiona wondered why Padruig wanted the *sgian dubh* he sought, and why he thought it would be here. He'd claimed Broc had taken things from Culloden Moor—Broc had gone to observe even if his wound had precluded him from fighting—but so might have many a man in the king's army.

"Sister," Broc said after he'd eaten his fill and drunk a little of the whisky. "I'm glad you are home."

"I am happy as well," Fiona said cautiously. It was a rare day Broc didn't follow a kind word with a demand.

"Tavin is right that I should go away from here. I doubt I'll ever have an heir." Broc had not married. The lady he'd set his eyes on had chosen another, and he'd nursed resentment and wounded pride in the five years since. "If you marry Tavin, you can both live here, and you'll bear the Macdonald heir."

Broc spoke woodenly, as though the speech was rehearsed. Fiona could guess who'd coached him.

She turned a sweet smile on Tavin who was trying to persuade Gair to hand him the whisky. Gair would begin to and then stop and pour more for himself or Padruig.

"No, thank you, Tavin," Fiona said clearly. "I will not marry you."

Tavin gave her a sour glance. "You might not have a choice, cousin. Broc won't sire any sons, thanks to his injury. You are his only hope. I am the logical man for you to marry. Neilan is the younger—he'll run our lands, while I take over here."

"Won't sire any sons?" Stuart's large rumble interrupted. "He was shot in the leg, not the balls. He'll sire sons just fine."

Broc's face went crimson. "Dinnae mock me, sir."

"Not mocking. 'Tis a fact. What have these idiots been filling your head with?"

"They talk a lot of sense," Broc said, though Fiona glimpsed a silent plea in his green eyes. "I won't be able to be laird much longer. A stronger man should take over."

"I see I came home just in time," Fiona began, but Stuart held up his hand.

"I crave a boon, Macdonald," Stuart said.

Broc flicked his tired gaze to him. "What?" He took a large sip of whisky, like a thirsty man who'd just found water.

"I'm searching for a *sgian dubh*. One lost on Culloden Moor. Do ye have such a thing? If ye can find it for me, I promise I'll rid ye of your unwanted guests and restore ye to your power."

CHAPTER 7

Broc frowned, more bewildered than interested. "A *sgian dubh*—?"

Padruig spoke the first words he'd uttered since they'd arrived. "Plain hilt. Crest of MacNab on it."

"I heard ye were light-fingered on that battlefield, Macdonald," Gair added. "Arrived to watch the slaughter and then retrieved weapons and things. Stashing them to bring home with ye."

Broc blinked. "Confiscating. They were the weapons of a fallen enemy and had to be secured."

Gair took a noisy sip of whisky. "Where did ye secure them to?"

"My strongroom. Until they're wanted. They'll be melted down, I think."

Padruig's silence was far more unnerving than Gair's snort. Stuart decided he'd better interrupt.

"It's one knife among many," Stuart said. "King Geordie will never miss it."

"They're not mine to give away—"

"They weren't yours t' take," Padruig said in his firm voice.

"Did ye hear my terms, Broc?" Stuart asked. "The *sgian dubh*, and your cousins vanish into the smoke and leave ye be. You are laird, you'll recover, find a bonny lass to marry ye, and have a score of bairns. These lummoxes have filled your head with tales."

"Now, look here—" Tavin began.

"God's balls, but ye sound like a Sassenach," Stuart growled. "Why don't ye take yourselves to England and have done?"

"We are *loyal* to England—to Britain." Tavin spoke as though he explained to a child. "We have land here, that we will keep arable or for sheep, and pay taxes we owe. In return, His Majesty leaves us alone. That's the sensible road to take these days. No popping white cockades on bonnets and believing the Stewart kings will rise again."

"Land, aye." Stuart nodded. He finished up his bannocks, which were crumbly and oat-y as he liked them. "But it's a lawless time. Ye never know what will happen to your lands if ye leave them for too long."

"That is why Neilan will go home and tend the estate," Tavin said patiently. "While I stay here and help Broc."

"Should go soon, the pair of ye," Stuart said. "I happen to know quite a few Highlanders not happy with those who turned on them. Ye never see them, but they're about. Wouldn't be surprised if ye find your fields burned, your houses taken down brick by brick, your tenants and retainers gone …"

Neilan looked nervous, but Tavin bristled.

"Marauders will be arrested, hanged as traitors and looters."

"If ye can catch them." Stuart calmly sipped whisky. "I know many men, throughout Scotland, and even England, in fact, who wouldn't mind stripping Hanoverian sympathizers of all they have."

"You never would," Tavin said, though he took on a note of uncertainty. "I'd arrest *you*."

"Oh, I won't go near your lands. Nothing to do with me." Stuart sent Fiona a wink.

Fiona gazed back at him, her eyes a beautiful green. She had no idea what he was doing, but her smooth face betrayed nothing.

Neilan spoke up. "What do you mean?" The silver snuffbox rested at his elbow, which meant Gair had successfully persuaded him to buy it.

Stuart leaned toward the cousins, enjoying himself. "Have ye never heard tell of the *brollachan* that did so much damage to the enemy camps during the Uprising? Oh, I beg your pardon, I mean loyalist camps, full of Highlanders happy to bow to King Geordie and pay him taxes."

"A *brollachan*?" Tavin scoffed. "Don't be daft. There is no such thing."

Neilan nodded, his eyes round. "I remember the tales."

"It was never a ghost," Tavin said loudly. "It was one of the Young Pretender's men playing tricks."

At that moment, a huge clatter sounded. Neilan leapt to his feet, and Tavin rose slowly. Broc jumped and stared. An empty pewter plate Gair had set on a smaller table had fallen for no apparent reason. Neilan gazed at it in terror, and Broc also looked stunned.

"Children's stories." Tavin resumed his seat with a thump. "Sit down, Neilan. Ye look like a half-wit."

Neilan resumed his seat, continuing to stare at the platter, as did Broc. Padruig, who'd knocked it to the floor while Stuart had held the cousins' attention, continued to eat.

"Mebbe." Stuart shrugged. "Whether 'tis men or ghosts, ye stand to lose everything. Can ye afford to? Is that the true reason you're here, trying to pick Broc's pockets?"

Neilan flushed guiltily, but Tavin bristled. "You're mad. If men are terrorizing the lands of loyalists, they'll be taken. Or shot."

"As I say, *if* ye can find them." Stuart tapped the side of his nose. "Now, I can put in a word for you with the *brollachan*, tell it to leave ye be."

"Because you're one of them?" Tavin asked. "Perhaps we'll have *you* arrested."

"'Twould be inhospitable," Stuart pointed out. "As I'm a guest in the house you wish to be yours."

Tavin began to splutter, but Fiona shushed him. She, like Padruig, had not jumped when the plate had fallen. It lay on the floor even now, the burnished pewter winking.

"It is an interesting point," Fiona said serenely. "Why the desire to take over Broc's lands, Tavin? Everything not well at home?"

"Of course everything is—"

"Stop lying." Neilan threw down his spoon and rounded on his brother. "We're skint. All our tenants ran off too. But everyone knows *ye* have the better lands, Broc. Tavin wants them. And Fiona. Notice it's me who has to stay home and try to eke out an existence while he takes over the laird's castle."

"Shut it, ye cretin." Tavin balled up his fist. Stuart reached across the table and caught Tavin's wrist before he could bash his brother.

Tavin extricated himself from Stuart's grip and sat down, red-faced. Neilan quickly rose and moved away from the table, coming to rest next to a stone pillar.

"I don't notice Fiona saying she'll marry ye," Neilan snarled at Tavin.

"A very good observation," Fiona said. "I turned you down a few minutes ago, Tavin, if you recall."

"You'll have to marry me." Tavin's polite affability disappeared. In its place was the hard ambition of a man who'd waited years to take what he wanted. "Look at Broc. He's dying, or as good as. He'll never walk right, never catch a bonny lass, as this lackey says, never have sons. You'll never command as a woman, Fiona, even if ye do become laird. Ye need the might of men behind ye, and they've all gone, haven't they? I'll take over as laird, and if you don't marry me, I'll turf ye out. You'll have nothing, nowhere to go. So ye have no choice, woman."

Fiona reached for her glass of whisky. "Ah, what a lovely proposal …"

Stuart's rage rose until his vision tinged with red. Tavin, with his round, pale face under the irritating wig, reminded him strongly of some officers Stuart had faced in battle, men who'd come out of their tents to fight only when they absolutely had to and then killed those who'd thrown up their hands in surrender.

"She'll not be marrying ye." Stuart's statement was flat, hard, and rang through the hall.

"Are ye going to stop her?" Tavin's smirk tempted Stuart to reach for the knife in his boot.

"Aye." He turned his gaze to Fiona, who had grown silent, her amusement gone. "Because she's marrying me." Stuart softened his voice as he held Fiona's stunned gaze. "If she'll have me."

The room went very quiet. Gair and Padruig ceased their noisy chewing and turned their way, interested.

Fiona's chest rose with her sharp breath. Stuart held his, waiting for her to laugh, to dismiss him with a wave, to say she needed no man. Fiona was a strong woman, who could stand on her own, no matter what her foolish family thought.

Fiona's eyes, the color of jade in sunshine, glistened in the lamplight.

"Yes," she whispered.

∽

Fiona's quiet word, which she said with all her heart, had a different effect on all present. Gair appeared highly amused, Tavin incensed, Neilan surprised, Broc shocked. Only Padruig remained stoic.

Stuart's grin spread across his face, her wild Highlander coming to life. He leapt from his seat, knocking the bench over behind him, and was around the table before Fiona could gasp.

He hauled her up and into his arms. "Ye mean it, love?"

Fiona clutched Stuart's coat, happiness flooding her.

This was *right*. She never should have let him go when he'd walked out a year and more ago, never been so complacent that she could see him whenever she wished.

She'd hang on now, wherever the road took them.

Tavin's hands landed on Stuart's shoulders. "Traitor! I'll kill you …"

The polished veneer Tavin strove to paste over his Highland ancestry had fled. His face was mottled red, his wig sliding sideways as he attacked the boulder that was Stuart.

Fiona ducked out of the way as Stuart swung on Tavin. Broc, to her astonishment, came to his feet and hobbled to Fiona, putting himself between her and the two fighting men. Protecting her.

Stuart lifted Tavin, crushing him between his large hands. Tavin flailed and fought. He must have studied pugilism somewhere, because his punches were tight and swift, each jab landing on Stuart's body.

Stuart flung Tavin away. Tavin stumbled but gained his feet, his wig falling to the floor to reveal his shaved head, dark with stubble. His face was twisted with a snarl, an enraged Highlander denied what he considered his.

Neilan stood stupefied as his brother toed off his impractical shoes and rushed Stuart. Stuart met Tavin in the middle of the wide room, a roar issuing from his throat. He must have yelled so at Prestonpans, where he'd captured English artillery, and again at Culloden, when he'd fought to the bitter end.

Tavin's arms flashed as he struck, Stuart defending blow after blow. Stuart was a larger man, but Tavin was quick and treacherous.

A knife flashed in Tavin's hand. Fiona cried out, but Stuart was already moving. He locked a strong grip around Tavin's wrist, bending the arm around Tavin's back. Tavin punched with his other fist, catching Stuart on the cheek, splitting it open. Blood spattered just as Tavin screamed, and Fiona heard a thin crack of bone.

The next instant, Tavin was on the floor, sobbing and hugging his arm, as Stuart kicked away the knife.

Stuart stood back, gathering his hair from his face, most of the soot having fallen away. The red gleamed in the half light, Stuart a grim giant over the fallen Tavin.

"You broke my arm, you bastard," Tavin ground out.

"Forgive me, lad." Stuart dragged in a long breath. "I'm tired of men sticking knives into me."

Fiona stepped from her brother and thrust a handkerchief at Stuart, who took it dazedly and touched it to his cut cheek. "Brawling in a laird's hall. I'm amazed at both of you."

Her voice shook, her bravado failing. She knelt next to Tavin and gently probed his arm. Tavin cursed and wept, the savage Highlander fading once more into the spoiled boy Tavin had always been.

"'Tis a clean break," Fiona said crisply. "I'll wrap and splint it for ye, and you'll be healed in a few weeks. I suggest ye go home and rest, and not venture out for a time."

"Aye, I'll take him." Neilan sounded relieved.

"I'm not leaving." Tavin scowled up at Fiona and Stuart. "Not until I have what I came for."

"My lands?" Broc stumped over, moving more quickly than Fiona had seen him do in a while, his stick ringing. "My home, my sister—everything? Get out,

Tavin. Ye're not welcome here. Go back to your house and stay there. I, as your laird, command it."

"Ye have no authority over me." Tavin's words were a gasp.

"Aye, that I do. I'm head of this family, and now that ye've shown your true colors, I'll do whatever I can to keep ye from inheriting. I'll marry whatever lass will have me and sire as many children as I've got years left in me."

Stuart's eyes twinkled with mirth over the blood-streaked handkerchief. "Better not say that when you're proposing, lad. Might put a lady off."

Broc ignored him. "On your feet, Tavin. Let Fiona see to your wound, and then you're gone."

Tavin finally looked worried. "In the night, and the snow? Have some pity, Broc. It's Christmas."

"'Tis not Christmas until tomorrow. I don't want ye here. Ye have a perfectly fine house ten miles away. Go before I find some way to throw you out of that too."

Tavin snarled. He swung his free hand at Fiona, but found it caught in Stuart's fist.

"I went easy on ye, lad." Stuart lowered his voice to deliver the warning. "But if ye try to hit Fiona again, I'll break every bone ye have."

Tavin gulped and subsided. Gair and Neilan emerged to flank Tavin. "Come on, you," Gair said, one hand under Tavin's arm. "Best ye retire from the scene of battle. I know how to set a broken bone."

Tavin threw a terrified glance at Gair and a beseeching one at Fiona. "Go with him," Fiona said "I'll be in to look after you soon."

Stuart released Tavin into Gair's care. Tavin had no

choice but to let Gair walk him out, Neilan quivering behind them.

Broc let out his breath. "I thank you, Stuart Cameron. I should never have let Tavin crawl under my skin. But I've been so afraid …"

Fiona slid her arm around her brother, and he leaned into her gratefully. "Never mind," she told him. "I'm sorry I stayed away so long this time. I didn't realize ye needed me."

"No, I drove ye from me." When Broc decided to become morose, he could be a master of it. "I'm glad ye returned, love. Stuart." Broc offered his hand, the other resting heavily on his stick. "Thank you. I am in your debt."

Stuart accepted the handshake, and he clapped Broc on the back. "Ye owe me nothing. Your blessing on my nuptials with Fiona and the *sgian dubh* I need, and all is cleared."

"I think Fiona will do well with you," Broc said graciously. "As for the *sgian dubh*, you are welcome to search through what I have found. If this knife is important, it should be returned to its owner."

He glanced at Padruig, who'd remained on the edge of the conflict and reunion. Broc shrank a little behind Fiona as Padruig gave him a keen look from his one sharp eye.

"I no longer need it," Padruig said.

Fiona blinked, startled. "Pardon?"

"Padruig," Stuart said with exaggerated patience. "What are ye talking about, man?"

"I have the *sgian dubh*." Padruig reached into his coat and removed a knife, holding it up to catch the light.

Fiona saw a plain dark steel blade, worn from years of use. The hilt was wrapped in a strip of leather, and a crest had been melded to it. Fiona clearly read the word *MacNab* on top of the shield.

Stuart growled. "How long have ye had that?"

"Since Culloden." Padruig calmly sheathed the knife and returned it to his pocket. "I took it from my dead brother."

Fiona caught her breath. "Your brother? Padruig, I'm so sorry."

"We were never close. But he was my kin." His nod at her sympathy said the matter was at an end.

Stuart's fists balled. "If ye have the blasted *sgian dubh*, why did ye give me the rigamarole about finding it for you? Making us search the lass's chamber at the inn, dragging us here? Through the snow? In the coldest part of December?"

"Ye needed to come here." Padruig flicked his gaze to Fiona. "*She* needed to. Ye were pining for her, Cameron. When I saw her at the inn, it put the idea in me mind."

Fiona shared Stuart's exasperation. "To trick us into traveling home?" she blurted out. "Did ye know my cousins were here?"

"No. That was luck." Padruig shrugged. "All's well, isn't it? You're betrothed and will soon be man and wife. And now that Stuart helped your brother, he'll not betray you." Padruig's lips twitched into a faint smile, something rare to his face. "Gair likened us to the three wise Highlanders, the daft sod. Come bearing gifts. This is my gift to you." He lifted his whisky glass. "*Slàinte.*"

He'd barely taken a sip before Fiona flew at him,

grabbing the startled Padruig in a hug and kissing his stubbly cheek.

"You're a wonderful, wonderful man." Fiona clasped his arm while Padruig peered down at her, his gaze softening. "Thank you."

CHAPTER 8

Stuart escorted Fiona up the stairs to the private chamber where Gair had retreated with Tavin —he could hear Tavin yelling all the way—to find that Gair had done a competent job of bandaging Tavin's arm.

Fiona studied Gair's work, ran skilled fingers over the splint, and nodded. "'Tis well done. You'll heal fine, cousin, so cease your wailing. Broc has kindly allowed you to stay the night, but you'll be off in the morning."

Stuart did not like the idea of Tavin spending one more evening in this house—what would he get up to, even injured? But Fiona, smiling sweetly, gave Tavin a thick liquid to drink, explaining it would ease his pain.

It must have eased it quite a lot, because after Tavin downed it, he slumped onto his brother, who reposed worriedly on the edge of the bed, and fell fast asleep. Gair, chuckling, retreated from the chamber and went back downstairs.

After a moment, they heard Gair's voice rise from below. "What? Ye bastard, ye dragged me across frozen

Scotland and nearly got me shot and ye had the bloody *sgian dubh* all along?"

"Shut it." Padruig's growl made Gair's bluster fade. "The whisky's good."

Gair trailed off into mutters, and Fiona smothered a laugh.

She rose, but her legs immediately folded, as though she'd drunk the potion she'd given Tavin.

Stuart caught her. "You're all in, love. Come with me."

With a curt good-night to Neilan, Stuart half-guided, half-carried Fiona up the next flight of steps to the rooms two floors above the hall. Here Broc and Fiona had their private chambers, spacious quarters high in the tower. The view, Stuart recalled, over the glens and to the mountains beyond, was worth the steep climb.

The vista was hidden by darkness now, the windows black. Stuart had been inside Fiona's sitting room before, and had kissed her in it, but he'd never ventured into the room beyond that, her bedchamber.

He took her there now, and Fiona did not stop him. The chamber held a tall bedstead with delicate posts— very modern—as well as brocade-upholstered chairs, a bookshelf filled with leather-bound tomes, a soft carpet, and hangings and paintings on the stone walls. Fiona had taken a cold room in an ancient stone castle and made it comfortable.

The fire had been lit, its small heat already permeating the room. Someone had turned down the bed as well, and Stuart saw the lump of heated bricks at the foot of it. The efficient Una, he guessed, looking after her mistress while the men brawled at the supper table.

Stuart shut the bedchamber door one-handed and clicked the key in the lock. "Lass."

Fiona turned in his arms, lacing hers around him. "Stuart."

Silence surrounded them as Stuart kissed her. Their lips met, parted, met again. Fiona loosened in his arms, her strength returning. She rested her hands on his back, and as he kissed her, she inched her touch down to his hips.

Stuart broke the kiss. "Lass." This time the word was tinged with laughter.

"I missed you." Fiona pulled him close. "I feared you gone forever."

"Nay." Stuart kissed her cheek, her throat. "I knew I had to live, to be free. To see my love again."

"Love?" The word warmed his ear.

"Aye." Stuart raised his head and cupped her face. "I love you, Fiona."

Fiona's answer was an unintelligible gargle as she launched herself at him. Her next kiss burned, her lips parting his. Stuart started when she suckled his tongue, then he deepened the kiss, letting her do what she would.

They were betrothed, in front of witnesses. No matter it hadn't yet been proclaimed to the world or announced at the nearest kirk. Fiona was his, and Stuart belonged to her.

Stuart slid off his coat, glad to be done with its weight. He unlaced Fiona's stomacher and eased her bodice open. Both of them wore many layers of clothing against the cold, and they came off one by one, the two of them starting to laugh as they unbuckled, unbuttoned, and untied endless garments.

Finally they stood together near the heat of the fire, body to body, nothing between them. Fiona traced his cheek.

"I love *you*, Stuart Cameron. Thank you for coming back to me."

"Ah, lass, I couldn't have stayed away from ye."

The next kiss erased all past sorrows. Stuart ran his hands down Fiona's pliant body, rejoicing in the silken smoothness of her skin.

He lifted her and carried her to the bed. Stuart climbed over her, and as the clock on the mantel chimed midnight, Stuart slid inside his love. His heart eased for the first time in a year, as Fiona's eyes softened, and she welcomed him.

Outside snow abraded the window, and inside, Christmas glided in amidst love and newfound joy.

∽

GAIR AND PADRUIG OFFERED TO ESCORT TAVIN AND Neilan home the next morning. Broc sent them off after a hearty breakfast that Una, Donia, and Fiona managed to create between them.

"He *is* a wise man," Fiona said as she and Stuart waved off the small party. The snow had ceased falling and lay in drifts under a clear blue sky. "Padruig, I mean."

"So he claims." Stuart sent Fiona a warm smile that trickled another frisson of desire through her.

She felt very different this morning, washed clean, and thoroughly loved. Fiona and Stuart had lain together throughout the night, drowsing at intervals before finding each other again. She'd wept in his arms, realizing anew how close she'd come to losing him. Stuart had kissed away her tears and held her with comforting strength.

"Will Gair and Padruig return, do you think?" Fiona asked.

"Probably not." Stuart guided her inside to the warmth of the main hall, Broc behind them. "Once Gair is paid, he vanishes. On to the next mark—I mean job."

"I heard him suggest they travel to a cove near Kilmorgan," Broc said. "And fetch their ship. Isn't that the seat of the Mackenzies?"

"It is," Stuart said. "Deserted now. But I imagine the Mackenzie brothers will find their way home. They always do."

Broc looked downcast. "I'd meant to pay you back by finding the *sgian dubh*. I was imagining presenting it in triumph."

"Take Padruig's gesture as a sign of peace between us," Stuart said. "All is well."

Fiona watched the two men shake hands, and impatience twinged her. "All is well? Nae so, Stuart Cameron. You're still a wanted man." She faced her brother. "If ye wish to pay back Stuart for ridding us of our greedy cousins, clear his name. Write to all your cronies in England and the army, and wherever else, and tell them Stuart is not to be touched. Say he was listed as a rebel by mistake. Something. Anything. I'm to marry the man—I don't want to worry the rest of my life that soldiers will come in the night and take him away."

Broc was already nodding as Fiona ran out of breath.

"It shall be done. I dinnae want my sister married to an outlaw either."

"Excellent. Shall we adjourn to your study so you can begin your letters?" Fiona took Broc firmly by the arm and turned him toward the stairs.

Stuart gave a shout of laughter. "Better do as she says, lad."

"Aye." Broc shot Stuart an ironic glance. "You see what you're marrying?"

"I do," Stuart said with warmth. "And I love her dearly for it. She truly is an angel of mercy."

Stuart's words and smile heated Fiona from head to toe. She guided her brother out, Stuart following, his laughter and his very presence the best Christmas gift she could have wished for.

EPILOGUE

TEN YEARS LATER

Hogmanay of 1756 arrived with all its bluster. Stuart Cameron gazed about the hall of his own house, which was filled with revelers.

When he and Fiona had reached the Cameron home the day after Christmas ten years ago, it had been as deserted and silent as he'd feared. But when word went out that Stuart had returned, his retainers and household staff emerged from all corners of the glen. They'd hidden after they'd heard of Stuart's capture and likely execution, but now reappeared to welcome home their laird and his new lady.

Ten years on, Stuart gazed across the wood-beamed ceiling at his wife, Fiona Cameron, who busily helped their oldest daughter, Alina, string garlands. A fiddler and a drummer practiced in the corner, ready to break into song. It was Hogmanay, and when the First-Footer arrived, the dancing would begin.

Alina, their first-born, looked so much like her mother, sharing her dark hair and green eyes. Likewise did their oldest son, who'd come two years later, Stuart Michael—they called him by his second name. The third son was Broc, named in honor of Fiona's brother. He was all Cameron, a strapping lad with bright red hair and blue eyes. Innis, the youngest daughter, also a redhead, had arrived two years ago. She played with empty spools at the moment, watched over by a smitten Una, the babe excited by the celebration.

Ten years of hope, happiness, and recovery. Ten years of love. The house was warm, full, laughter and music echoing from every corner. Broc had kept his promise and had used his influence in the government and military to clear Stuart's name. No more fear of the Butcher's men chasing him through every corner of the country. When Malcolm Mackenzie had been restored to the dukedom of Kilmorgan, he had added his assistance to make certain Stuart, the Mackenzies' old friend, lived undisturbed. Even so, Fiona and her network of ladies had continued aiding Highlanders who needed to flee Scotland, and Stuart had been happy to help her.

Broc had found a lass for himself—not a sad dowager who'd leap at the chance to marry any man, as he'd feared, but a fine woman with fire in her eyes. She'd nursed Broc back to health and borne him three dark-haired sons. Broc had been transformed.

Tavin and Neilan had wisely decided to try their luck in France, and had departed Scotland's shores, so far never to return. Broc, as their nearest relative and their laird, had taken over their property, keeping it in trust for his younger sons.

Fiona swirled by, stooping to kiss Stuart on the lips. His body stirred, craving another morning like this one had been, he with Fiona in their large bed, wrapped around each other.

Fiona winked at him as she hurried on, knowing his thoughts.

"The First-Footer!" Michael shouted as someone pounded on the massive door below.

He and his brother raced down the stairs. Stuart caught up Innis and followed, Fiona and Una coming after him with Alina.

The clocks were striking twelve. If the first guest in the door had dark hair, they'd have good luck all the year. If he or she were blond …

Michael, impatient, shoved open the bolts. A man, slight and small with white-gray hair pushed inside, snow swirling after him.

"About time ye opened up. Me balls will freeze off."

"Gair!" Fiona eyed him reproachfully even as she pulled him inside. "You're the First-Footer. It was supposed to be Broc or one of his sons."

"He's pulling his children off the horses—takes him a while." Gair beamed a broad smile. "'Tis no matter. Me hair was black as tar when I was a boy."

"Very well," Fiona said, resigned. "Upstairs to the hall with you. But nothing goes in your pockets, mind."

Gair widened his eyes. "I don't know what you mean."

Padruig pushed in behind him. "Shut it, Gair." He turned his gray eye to Fiona. "I'll watch over him."

Padruig and Gair appeared scarcely any different. Same weather-beaten faces, same scruffy clothes. But they'd filled out, well-fed, and their coats, though salt-crusted from the sea and mud-spattered from their journey, were of fine brocade and velvet. Rumor had it that they'd stumbled across a treasure—possibly even the French gold that was supposed to have come to aid Prince Teàrlach. No one could confirm this rumor, and Gair and Padruig had never mentioned it to a soul.

"*You* are welcome," Fiona said to Padruig. "As always."

Padruig gave her a nod. "Thank ye, lass." He handed her a small silk bag that clinked. "A gift for ye and your wee ones."

Fiona took the bag with a smile, loosened its drawstrings, and peered inside. Her face lost color. "Padruig …" she said in awe.

Padruig closed her hand over the bag. "Never ask."

"Of course not." She slid the bag into her pocket.

The fiddles and drums upstairs began to play. Broc, with his wife and children, sailed through the door, Broc no longer needing the stick to hold him upright. A slight limp was all that was left of his wound from Falkirk.

Fiona hugged him and her sister-in-law and nephews. Amidst the greetings she took her children's hands and led everyone upstairs while music poured around them.

"A fine Hogmanay," she called above the fiddles to Stuart. "Complete with my three wise Highlanders."

Stuart leaned to her. "And my bonny wife. I love ye, Fiona Cameron."

"I love you too, Stuart."

The drums sped, the fiddles played, and Stuart swept his wife and children into the first dance, his world complete.

"And they lived happily ever after."

Ian Mackenzie concluded the story with the expected phrase, and Megan sighed happily.

Ian had become aware, as he told the tale, that the other Mackenzie children, Ian's brothers, and Beth had crept in to listen. Jamie, his son, as unlike Ian as could be—thankfully, in Ian's opinion—was the first to ask questions. This was usual.

"MacNab. The name on Padruig's *sgian dubh*. Wasn't the mum of Old Malcolm Mackenzie a MacNab?"

"Allison MacNab, aye." Ian gave him a slow nod. "She was Padruig's kinswoman. Distant. In the same clan."

"Did Gair and Padruig really have the French gold?" Ian's oldest daughter, Belle, asked.

Ian shrugged. "So Will Mackenzie believed. Fiona's journal doesn't say what was in the bag Padruig gave her."

"It was some of the gold," Jamie declared. "I'm sure of it."

"How can you know?" Belle asked. "If no one has said for certain?"

"Because Gair and Padruig were old scoundrels. Of course they wouldn't confess they had all the gold from the French king." Jamie's older-brother scoff was firm.

Belle, who had plenty of fire, began to argue. The discussion was taken up by other Mackenzies, including Ian's brothers Mac and Cameron, all having an opinion to share.

Ian let them go on while his gaze went to Beth, her blue eyes shining in merriment.

Ian enjoyed the stories of the past, when his ancestors

had fought to survive, using cunning and craftiness to keep themselves and their families safe. They'd lived and loved with intensity in a time when Scotland had been untamed.

As Ian glanced about the full room, he decided that as interesting as the past must have been, now was better. Ian was surrounded by his family and his wife—who loved him and whom he loved back with vehemence.

They'd saved his life, especially Beth, who bent down to kiss his cheek. She'd made certain Ian could sit in peace, surrounded by warmth and love.

That was the truest gift of all.

~

THANK YOU FOR READING! THIS NOVELLA IS A PART OF the Mackenzies / McBrides series, which begins with ***The Madness of Lord Ian Mackenzie***. For more information on this series and others, see my website:

https://www.jenniferashley.com

More Mackenzies to come!

ALSO BY JENNIFER ASHLEY

Historical Romances

Regency Bon Bons

(short, sweet Regencies)

A First-Footer for Lady Jane

Duke in Search of a Duchess

A Kiss for Luck

The Mackenzies Series

The Madness of Lord Ian Mackenzie

Lady Isabella's Scandalous Marriage

The Many Sins of Lord Cameron

The Duke's Perfect Wife

A Mackenzie Family Christmas: The Perfect Gift

The Seduction of Elliot McBride

The Untamed Mackenzie

The Wicked Deeds of Daniel Mackenzie

Scandal and the Duchess

Rules for a Proper Governess

The Stolen Mackenzie Bride

A Mackenzie Clan Gathering

Alec Mackenzie's Art of Seduction

The Devilish Lord Will

A Rogue Meets a Scandalous Lady

A Mackenzie Yuletide

Fiona and the Three Wise Highlanders

Historical Mysteries

Kat Holloway "Below Stairs" Victorian Mysteries

(writing as Jennifer Ashley)

A Soupçon of Poison

Death Below Stairs

Scandal Above Stairs

Death in Kew Gardens

Murder in the East End

Death at the Crystal Palace

ABOUT THE AUTHOR

New York Times bestselling and award-winning author Jennifer Ashley has written more than 100 published novels and novellas in romance, urban fantasy, mystery, and historical fiction under the names Jennifer Ashley, Allyson James, and Ashley Gardner. Jennifer's books have been translated into more than a dozen languages and have earned starred reviews in *Publisher's Weekly* and *Booklist*. When she isn't writing, Jennifer enjoys playing music (guitar, piano, flute), reading, hiking, and building dollhouse miniatures.

More about Jennifer's books can be found at
http://www.jenniferashley.com

To keep up to date on her new releases, join her newsletter here:
http://eepurl.com/47kLL

Printed in Great Britain
by Amazon